MAYDAY!

MAYDAY!

Dan Stratman

MAYDAY!

ISBN: 978-1-7325992-0-8 (print)
ISBN: 978-1-7325992-1-5 (eBook)

Published by:
Flying D Publishing LLC

ACKNOWLEDGMENTS

A lot of kind people helped me turn my scribblings into a book I am proud of. I want to thank: Jan Stratman, Luellen, Phil Hefley, Jeff Desilets, Rick Henderson, Chris Brandt, members of the Astronomical Society of Kansas City, Cary Jackson, Heather Shinn, and Dr. Jim Singer.

A special thanks to my editor Jason Whited. You rock!

DEDICATION

To my dear sweet wife Cyndi, the best wife and mother to our children a guy could ask for. As it turns out, one heck of an editor as well.

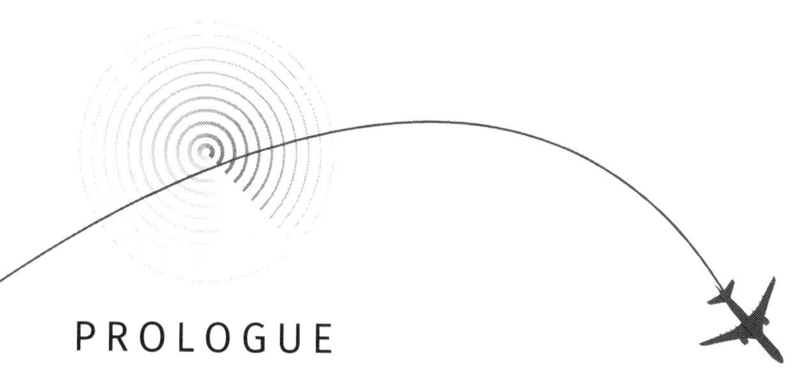

PROLOGUE

FIFTY YEARS AGO

THE JERSEY SHORE was sweltering that Fourth of July. Hank Smith sat alone on his tattered, olive-green army blanket that was spread out haphazardly on the hot sand. Between swigs of cheap beer, he stared glassy-eyed at the waves as they rolled in. Seagulls lazily circled overhead, looking for an opportunity to swoop down and steal food from unsuspecting tourists.

Nearby, two blonde, bikini-clad sorority girls strolled down the overcrowded beach arm in arm, laughing and gossiping about boys. When they crossed his field of vision, Hank stuck the ends of two fingers in his mouth and let out a loud, crass wolf whistle.

The girls turned excitedly to search for their admirer. They were shocked to see a hairy, forty-two-year-old man with a bad comb-over and a beer belly lapping over his Speedo waving at them. Repulsed, they looked at each other and squealed, "Eewww, gross!"

Hank hoisted his beer can in a mock toast and yelled, "Cheers!" Under his breath he muttered, "Bitches." Rejected again by the fairer sex, he tilted his head back and drained the last drop from the can. Hank crushed it and tossed the empty can on a growing pile, making it an even dozen. Grabbing another beer from the cooler, he swiped it across his sweaty brow, trying to counter the effects of the thick, humid air.

With his leathery hand, Hank shaded his eyes from the glare of the sun and scanned the beach. He saw a scrawny boy headed his way. The boy was playing with a toy airplane, making loud jet engine noises as he swooped the plane up, down, left, and right.

Hank cupped his hands around his mouth and yelled, "Mark!"

Lost in his own world, the boy didn't hear the call.

"Marcus Daniel Smith!" Hank yelled louder.

The boy stopped and looked up.

"Get your ass over here!"

The boy landed the pretend flight and ran over, clutching his prized toy.

"Where the hell have you been?" Hank scolded him. "I've been looking all over for you."

"I thought you could see me," Mark protested. He pointed thirty feet down the beach. "I was just over there."

"Next time tell me before you go running off like that."

"Sorry, Dad." Mark's head dropped.

Regretting the undeserved scolding, Hank tried to make amends. He patted the worn blanket. "Sit down here next to your old man and keep me company."

Knowing all too well the consequences of angering his father in his current state, Mark reluctantly plopped down on the far edge of the tattered blanket.

A few minutes of awkward silence passed. Hank polished off another can. Bored, Mark ran his finger through the sand, drawing random shapes. As Hank grabbed another beer, he looked over and pointed at the plane. "What ya got there?"

Mark's eyes lit up. "It's a Boeing 707! The best airplane in the whole world! It goes seven million miles an hour and can fly all the way from New York to—"

"You and your airplanes. Don't you ever think about anything else?"

Mark's enthusiasm immediately drained away.

Oblivious to his son's feelings, Hank continued. "What about girls? You got any girlfriends yet?"

"Daaaddd! I'm only ten."

"You're ten already?" Hank was genuinely surprised. Any guilt he felt about the shortcomings of his parenting slipped from Hank's mind faster than sand through an open hand. Returning the focus to himself, Hank boasted,

"Hell, when I was your age I had a different girlfriend for every day of the week."

Mark looked like he had just bitten into a lemon. "Girls are yucky."

"Yucky?" Hank chuckled, then stopped and thought about his own past experience. "You can say that again," he snorted. Hank inhaled a deep breath of the salty sea air. "Enough about girls. Come on, let's go for a swim."

Mark looked over at the pile of beer cans—a familiar sight—and shook his head. "Can we go home now? I'm tired."

"Tired? I bring you all the way to the beach on the one day I get you, and you don't even want to go swimming?" Hank looked at Mark with a skeptical eye. "You're not scared of the water, are you?"

"No. I just want to go home," Mark fibbed.

"Bull. You're just scared, that's all. No son of mine is going to grow up to be a damned chicken. I know how to fix that. Same way my old man did." Hank scooped up Mark, threw him over his shoulder and waded waist-deep out into the warm ocean.

Mark banged his tiny fists on his dads back. "Let me down! I don't want to go in the water! Please, let me down!"

Ignoring his son's pleas, Hank lifted Mark off his shoulder and tossed him into the ocean like an empty beer can.

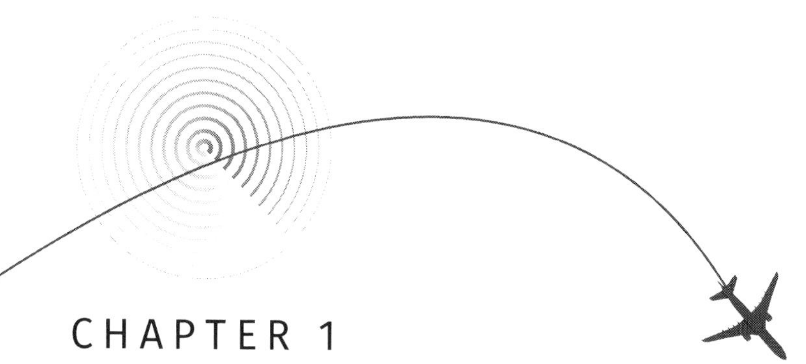

CHAPTER 1

PRESENT DAY

A PICTURE POSTCARD view of the dazzling lights of Broadway and Times Square illuminated the darkened cockpit as the pilots lined up to land at John F. Kennedy International Airport.

Ignoring the view, the copilot looked over jealously at his captain in the left seat. "So, two weeks in Maui. Nice. What's the special occasion?"

"I'm surprising the wife for our twenty-fifth anniversary," the captain bragged.

A radio call interrupted their conversation. "Alpha Flight 347, JFK tower, cleared to land runway one three left. You're starting to catch the plane in front of you. Slow down now to your final approach speed."

The copilot keyed his microphone. "Roger. Cleared to land. Slowing now."

The captain pulled the throttles back to idle and disengaged the autopilot. "Gear down. Flaps full," he commanded.

The chatty copilot extended the landing gear and wing flaps. "Twenty-five years? You must still be on number one," he joked.

"Yep, original model. Twenty-five years of marital bliss. Well, twenty-five years, at least. I figured after putting up with me for all those years, the least I could do is take her to a nice resort."

"That's gonna set you back a few bucks. Where are you staying?"

"I got a hell of a deal at the Grand Wailea Resort, right on the beach. It's got a swim-up bar and a—"

"STALL!"

"STALL!"

"STALL!"

The startled pilots' brains were barraged with blaring warning messages and flashing red lights indicating a dangerously low airspeed. The copilot's younger brain cells recognized the cause of the warnings a millisecond before the captain's. "Full power! Full power!" he screamed.

The captain grabbed the throttle levers and slammed them full forward. Superhuman strength gained from the massive shot of adrenalin suddenly coursing through his veins, caused the metal levers to bend. Then he made a fatal mistake. Frightened by the ground rushing up at him, the captain pulled back on his control yoke.

Before the engines had a chance to spool up to full power, the cockpit shuddered violently—the sign of a deep stall. Suddenly, the right wing dropped as the plane snap-rolled into an inverted spin. Upside down, the plane plunged from the night sky above a neighborhood full of densely packed brownstones.

The pilots knew they were too low to attempt a recovery from the spin. Instinctively, they crossed their arms in front of their faces as if doing so would protect them from harm.

One second before the doomed airliner obliterated the defenseless neighborhood, the view out the cockpit windows froze.

Lights in the cockpit came on, illuminating the shell-shocked look on the pilots' faces.

The instructor pilot leaned forward and barked, "Congratulations, gentlemen. One radio call from me, while you chatterboxes discussed what color umbrellas you want in your mai tais, and you stalled the plane, killed everyone on board, and who knows how many innocent people on the ground. You're both grounded. I want to see you in my office tomorrow morning at 8 a.m. sharp."

With that, Capt. Mark Smith stood up and stormed out the door at the back of the simulator.

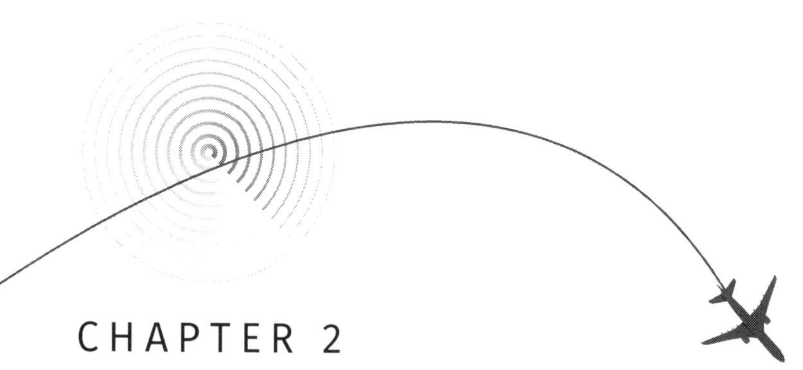

CHAPTER 2

THE NEXT AFTERNOON

OVER ONE MILLION pounds of aluminum, highly flammable fuel, oblivious passengers, and barely edible food roared down the runway, quickly picking up speed.

The scalding jet exhaust, a broiling 750 degrees Celsius, caused the air behind the airliner to ripple like a desert mirage. Eventually, the Boeing 747 lumbered off the two-mile-long strip of concrete at JFK, thumbing its nose at gravity.

The heavy jumbo jet struggled upward into the bitter January sky as it headed off to some balmy, tropical destination. As it ascended, the plane passed over a rusting and worn hangar—world headquarters of Alpha Airlines. The company's ultramodern red-white-and-blue logo was proudly mounted above the dented hangar door. Wisps of windblown snow swirled across the dirty concrete, accumulating in gray piles of slush at the edge of the tarmac.

When the jet engine noise faded away, a snappy rendition of *Birdland* could be heard coming from behind the closed hangar doors.

INSIDE THE LARGE hangar, the normally grimy space had been lavishly redecorated to resemble a glitzy Las Vegas casino. A casino with the strong smell of jet fuel.

A temporary stage was set up on the oil-stained floor, along with hundreds of chairs for the occasion. A twelve-piece jazz ensemble, nattily dressed in white tuxedoes, sat off to the side of the stage playing favorites by Weather Report, Miles Davis, and Billie Holiday. To the consternation of the band leader, the terrible acoustics caused the music to reverberate incessantly inside the metal-walled echo chamber.

Behind the stage, a dozen stone-faced security guards stood in front of an enormous black floor-to-ceiling curtain, preventing the crowd from sneaking a peek behind it. In front of the stage, a select assembly of people in formal attire representing all the economic powerhouses of the world mingled in a roped-off VIP section. A group of young Silicon Valley techies dressed casually in hoodies and obscure alternative rock band T-shirts were a conspicuous exception.

Waiters and waitresses dressed as flight attendants circulated among the VIPs, serving them bubbling flutes of Dom Pérignon and hot hors d'oeuvres from silver platters.

The general public, standing outside of the ropes, got nothing.

THE LARGE AUDIENCE was now seated, eagerly waiting for the presentation to begin. The jazz ensemble enthusiastically played another song from their repertoire. A row of chairs, occupied by corporate types in suits, lined the back edge of the stage. One token airline captain, signified by four gold stripes at the end of each sleeve on his jacket, sat in the last chair.

A trim, distinguished-looking man in his early sixties stepped up to the podium to speak. His fake tan was noticeably out of place in the middle of the winter.

The band played on.

He waited, forcing a smile, hands firmly planted on his hips.

The band continued to play.

The man lifted his chin and drew his finger sideways across his throat, sending a clear message.

Like the game of musical chairs, the band leader stopped the music in mid-note.

The speaker smiled broadly and said, "Good afternoon and welcome to today's ceremony. My name is Ralph Sanders. For the few of you that don't recognize me, I'm the CEO of Tech Aerospace Corporation. On behalf of everyone at Tech Aero, I want to thank Alpha Airlines for asking me to preside over this momentous occasion." Always looking out for the bottom line, he added, "Of course, a very special welcome to any potential future customers of our fabulous planes in the audience." Waving the wait staff toward the VIPs, Sanders said, "Give them all the champagne they want. It's on me." His paltry attempt at incentivizing the affluent crowd to buy his multimillion-dollar planes fell flat.

Even after years of grueling development, supply chain glitches, and billions of dollars of company money spent, the FAA had the ultimate say whether a new airliner got certified as safe to fly. Fully aware of that fact, Sanders sucked up to the leader of the agency. "We are especially honored to have our wonderful FAA administrator, Michael Hernandez, joining us today." He pointed back at the young, handsome man. Despite Sanders's gushing introduction, there was a slight tinge of disdain in his voice. The disdain betrayed his opinion that the young political appointee was way out of his depth and didn't even have the sense to realize it.

Hernandez flashed a big smile and gave the crowd a politician's wave.

Sanders got back to business. "They said it couldn't be built. Too advanced, they said. So, we brought in the best minds in Silicon Valley to work alongside our top engineers." He pointed at the techies. They turned and high-fived each other. One stood up and took a thank-you bow.

Sanders continued. "The end result of all our hard work? An aviation masterpiece. The most computerized, fully integrated, technologically advanced airliner ever conceived." He beamed as he added, "Heck, even the toilets are controlled by computers on our plane." Sweeping his hand back toward the curtain, he dramatically pronounced, "Ladies and gentlemen, I give you... the Tech-Liner!"

The hangar went dark.

The rap song "Get Ready for This" blasted from the speakers. White smoke from a fog machine blanketed the floor. Multiple spark cannons fired a shower of white-hot sparks into the air. The crowd started clapping and moving rhythmically to the beat.

If the crowd had thought about their surroundings, they should have been running for their lives. Strong jet fuel fumes plus spark cannons?

The enormous curtain fell to the floor revealing a gleaming new, twin-engine jumbo jet. Its sleek, futuristic design made it look like it was going Mach 2 just sitting in the hangar. With a wingspan of 250 feet and a length of 225 feet, the Tech-Liner was massive—by far the largest plane ever to grace the old hangar. A newly designed GE125 engine, the largest and the most powerful jet engine ever built, dangled under each wing. The enormous engine looked big enough to swallow a whole city bus in one gulp. Alpha Airlines logo was proudly displayed on the soaring tail. A tail that had been measured three times to make sure it would fit under the hangar doorframe.

Multicolored spotlights waved around frenetically, creating a garish Las Vegas atmosphere. A chorus line of sexy dancers dressed in skimpy flight attendant-style outfits strode onto the floor. They bumped and ground in unison to the thumping beat like cheerleaders for an NBA team.

Up on the stage, Sanders tried to look cool by boogying to the music. His attempt failed.

The show ended with a blinding flash of light and a loud BOOM.

"Woo! How 'bout that! Isn't she a beauty?" Sanders gushed. "And wait until you see the inside." Sanders straightened his tie. "I can't tell you how proud I am of my team. Great job, guys. Now let me introduce someone whom I've come to know and admire during the long development process of our plane. Mike Andrews is our host today and the CEO of Alpha Airlines. Mike was pivotal in making Alpha Airlines the launch customer for our new Tech-Liner. Please welcome Mike to the podium."

Andrews walked up with the swagger of a fighter pilot. The glaring disparity between his cocky gait and his slovenly appearance caused some in the audience to chuckle under their breath. Halfhearted, obligatory clapping greeted the dumpy middle-aged oaf of a man as he arrived at the podium.

Sanders vigorously shook Andrews's hand. "Mike, on behalf of all 80,000 employees at Tech Aerospace, I want to thank you for your unwavering trust in us. I present to you the key to Alpha Airline's first Tech-Liner." Sanders handed him a large, tacky cardboard key.

The two turned toward the press and engaged in a long photo-op handshake, smiling for the cameras. Andrews turned his back to the crowd and said in a low voice only the two of them could hear, "This thing better live up to the hype, or I'm yanking the entire order." The two men continued to smile and shake hands. Sanders got the message from his largest customer. With a forced smile plastered on his face, he sat down.

In the blink of an eye, Andrews did a Dr. Jekyll-like transformation back to friendly CEO. "Thank you, Ralph. I've enjoyed working with you as well."

Holding up the cardboard key, he joked, "What, no key ring?" When the anticipated laughs didn't come, Andrews continued. "Seriously, we are thrilled to be the launch customer of this fabulous plane. It represents my vision for Alpha Airlines: Be first. Be the best. That's why I've committed my airline to its largest aircraft order in our history—seven *billion* dollars—for a fleet of Tech-Liners."

In the crowd, members of the International Association of Machinists and Aerospace Workers, Local 1987, burst into applause.

Shifting gears, Andrews said, "The inaugural flight of our new plane this evening will be under the command of our chief pilot, Capt. Mark Smith." Andrews pointed back at the lone pilot on the stage. "Mark, stand up."

Mark reluctantly stood up and gave a half wave to the crowd.

From a distance, Mark's broad shoulders, sturdy six-foot-two frame, and just the right amount of pewter-gray hair to inspire confidence made him the quintessential pilot with the "right stuff." A closer look into his seafoam-green eyes revealed a different person entirely: someone tired, lonely, and worn down from life's many wounds.

That hadn't always been the case. As a young US Air Force pilot, Mark had had a sparkle in his green eyes and the type of roguish good looks that attracted women in droves—attributes that made him very popular among fellow pilots when out partying. Eventually, he had to choose his long-term career path. So, a lifetime ago, Mark left the Air Force after his commitment was up and got a "real" job flying for the airlines. Not as exciting as flying supersonic, upside down, at five hundred feet, but calmer. Calm being a relative term when used to describe the volatile airline industry. An industry that wears down even the hardiest of souls.

"Captain Smith is our most experienced and trusted pilot. Rest assured, you will be in good hands. So please, enjoy the buffet while we get the plane ready for its maiden flight to London. Soon we'll be ready to light this candle!" The aviation-savvy audience members audibly groaned at the plagiarized Alan Shepard quote.

Andrews walked over to Mark and halfheartedly shook his hand. Mark wasn't amused at being used as a prop. "Light this candle? Really?"

Andrews snapped, "Look here, Smith, I've got a lot riding on this trip. I can't tolerate any problems."

"Relax, I'll make it a memorable one," Mark assured him.

"See to it that you do." Then Andrews spitefully added, "You were damn lucky your union was able to get you back in the cockpit. This is your last trip, Smith. Don't screw it up." Andrews achieved his goal with that last crack—getting under Mark's skin.

Mark felt his blood pressure rapidly rising. He fumed inside at his boss for throwing that dark period from his past in his face. Yes, he had been lucky to get his job back after hitting rock bottom four years ago. If it hadn't been for the union going to bat for him too many times to count, Mark would have been fired long ago. But that was the distant past. During rehab, Mark learned to swallow his pride and took full responsibility for his drinking. He cleaned up his act and had been sober ever since. As far as Mark was concerned, his internal demons were pretty much under control.

Now all he wanted to do was fly to London without anyone dredging up his past mistakes—especially Mike Andrews. Before his temper got the better of him, Mark said, "If you'll excuse me, Mr. Andrews, I need to go do my flight planning." Mark quickly made his exit down the stairs on the side of the stage.

As he waded through the large crowd swarming around the shiny new plane to get a closer look, a young boy broke loose from his father's hand and ran up to Mark. "Are you a policeman?" the boy said, with awe in his voice.

The embarrassed father quickly stepped in and apologized. "Sorry, sir. He saw your uniform and thought..."

Mark understood. "No problem; don't worry about it." Looking at the boy, Mark said in a teacher-like voice, "See that big plane behind you? I fly that." Mark reached into his pocket and handed the boy a set of plastic pilot wings. "Here you go. You have to have wings if you want to fly one of those when you get bigger."

The boy held the prized wings right up to his father's face. "Wow, cool! Look, Dad!"

Mark joked with the boy. "Say, if my copilot doesn't show up tonight, can your dad help me fly my plane?"

"No, he'd better not," the boy responded, in all seriousness.

Mark cocked his head. "Why's that?"

In the type of honesty that only springs from the young, the boy blurted out, "My mom said if he gets one more speeding ticket, she's going to—"

The embarrassed father jumped in. "OK! Let the pilot get back to his duties, Son." He quickly maneuvered his offspring toward the exit with a hand on each shoulder. Before moving on, the father leaned over toward Mark. "Thanks for taking the time sir. You made his day."

"Happy to do it. I was that age once." Mark smiled as he recalled his own infatuation with airplanes as a boy.

The boy looked back as he was led away and waved at Mark with a big toothless grin.

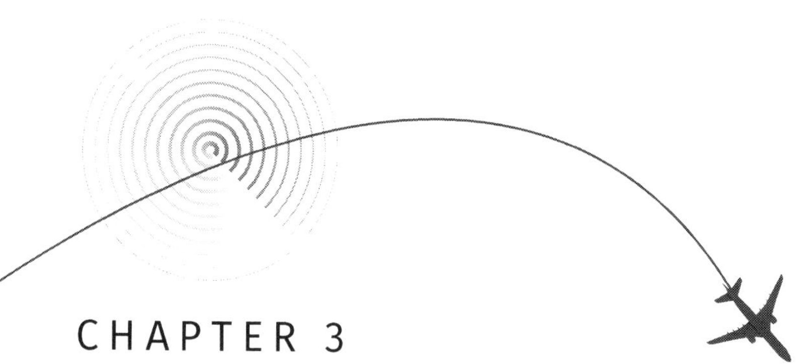

CHAPTER 3

EVENING HAD FALLEN, and the public was long gone. The stage and flamboyant decorations had been removed and the hangar reverted to its normal grimy state.

Three mechanics in dirty coveralls rolled portable boarding stairs up to the Tech-Liner's passenger door. In a nod to the region known for cutting-edge technology (as well as Google Glasses), *Spirit of Silicon Valley* was proudly painted on the side of the nose.

Maintenance Supervisor Tony Russo led his team up the stairs. Short, stocky, and olive-skinned, he was the poster boy for a Brooklyn Italian.

Following the boss was Marvin Timmons. After hauling his 320-pound frame up the stairs, Timmons stopped to catch his breath. Between gasps for air, he looked back down the stairs and barked, "Hurry up, rookie."

Bringing up the rear was the junior man on the team, Ahmed Harris. Ahmed lagged as he dutifully lugged a heavy tool box up the stairs.

The mechanics walked into the passenger cabin and were met with that distinctive new car smell, albeit that of an extraordinarily expensive new car. Every inch of the posh interior was perfect. The virgin airliner would never look as pristine or smell this good again. But start earning its keep, it must. Still, it was almost a shame to let tank-top- and flip-flop-wearing passengers mess it up.

The mechanics walked past widely spaced rows of plush seats covered in soft, cream-colored leather and trimmed with gold. Each first-class seat was its own luxury retreat with every creature comfort imaginable: HD video screens, built-in massage, heat, and the ability to fold down into a comfy twin-size bed. The spacious cabin was arranged with one seat next to each window and two seats between the double aisles. No need to worry about bruised kneecaps from the seat in front on this flight.

Russo looked around and said in his thick Brooklyn accent, "She's a beauty, ain't she?"

Timmons frowned, then grumbled. "Better be. The damned company paid for it with *our* money, that they stole from *our* friggin' pensions."

Russo tried to reason with him. "Move on, man. Yeah, we got hosed. The pricks took my pension, too. But the bankruptcy was five years ago. Let it go."

Timmons resented having his retirement dreams stolen by the greedy bastards. "I'll move on when those crooks get put in the slammer!"

Russo shook his head and walked off. "Good luck with that."

THE WRENCH BENDERS entered the roomy, futuristic cockpit. The "front office" of the Tech-Liner was anything but a typical airliner cockpit. It looked like a cross between the cockpit of the Space Shuttle and the bridge of the Starship Enterprise. Three multifunction touch screens were mounted side by side, spanning the entire width of the instrument panel. The normal jungle of buttons, switches, indicator lights, and "steam" gauges that covered every inch of older airliner cockpits were gone. On the Tech-Liner most were represented virtually on the screens. And unlike most airliners, there was no control yoke that extended up from the floor in front of each pilot. When the pilots wanted to hand-fly the plane, they used a computer game-style joystick located on the outboard panels under each side window.

Russo slipped into the clean captain's seat in his dirty overalls. He slid a work table out from under the bottom of the instrument panel and locked it in front of himself. Russo needled Timmons before getting started with his preflight duties. "How 'bout that game last week? My Giants kicked your Cowboys' asses. Pay up, loser."

Searching for a way to welch on his bet, Timmons whined, "Puh-leeze, they got lucky. The refs were in the tank the whole game."

Russo should have known better than to expect his bitter coworker to make good. "Yeah, yeah, blame the refs. You still owe me two Gs. Just gimme the computer, ya loser."

Timmons opened a gray metal case labeled CONTROLLED ITEM, BRAIN KIT #1 in bold red letters. He removed a laptop computer from the protective foam and handed it to his supervisor. Russo laid it on the work table and turned it on. The computer clicked and whirred to life. He typed in the maintenance department password then logged in to the plane's Wi-Fi network.

The other piece of equipment in the case was an electronic module the size of a cigarette pack—the "Brain."

Timmons carefully lifted the module from the foam cutout, walked to the back of the cockpit, and opened a small hatch door on the floor.

Before Timmons could start down the opening, Ahmed snatched the Brain out of his hand. "Gimme that thing. You'll never fit your fat ass through the hatch." He quickly descended the ladder before his coworker could stop him.

Thinking Ahmed might be right, but loath to admit it, Timmons threatened, "Watch it, punk, or I'll lock your ass down there for good!"

THE HOT, CRAMPED electronics compartment under the cockpit was a maze of computers, power supplies, and black boxes with their functions stenciled in white letters on the front. The acrid, metallic smell of hot circuit boards filled the air.

Ahmed could barely squeeze his way along a narrow walkway between the racks of equipment. Safely away from his abusive coworker, he summoned up the courage to yell, "See, I was right! Fat ass." Ahmed opened a clear plastic cover on the face of a computer and plugged the Brain into a recessed slot. As soon as a connection was made, indicator lights on the end of the module rapidly blinked. "OK, go ahead!" he yelled back toward the hatch.

RUSSO PULLED UP an aircraft preflight test program on the laptop. What used to take a team of mechanics an hour—checking over all the systems on a plane before each flight—now took one minute. After clicking EXECUTE, a virtual representation of the three cockpit screens came up on the laptop. The cockpit instrumentation displayed on the virtual screens simulated the plane being airborne at thirty-five thousand feet. The same picture popped up on the actual cockpit screens. The laptop program automatically cycled the systems on the plane through various tests: communication, navigation, flight controls, engines. The throttles moved full forward, then back to idle. Both pilots' joysticks moved by themselves, as if possessed. The fly-by-wire computer system instantly sensed the stick movements. On the outside of the plane, the ailerons, rudder, and elevators moved full travel in each direction.

A green TEST SUCCESSFUL banner popped up on the laptop screen. Russo typed a few more entries into the laptop then yelled, "All right, Ahmed, it passed!" He closed the laptop and handed it back to his coworker.

Timmons carefully placed the laptop back in the protective foam. "You gonna sign off the logbook?"

"Yep. She's good to go."

Timmons passed Russo a thick aircraft logbook containing records of all maintenance performed on the plane since it was built. Until the maintenance supervisor signed it off as safe to fly, the plane was nothing more than a very expensive paperweight in the regulatory eyes of the FAA. Russo scribbled his approval in the logbook page then ripped out the carbon copy below.

Ahmed poked his head out of the hatch, holding the Brain.

Timmons got even by snatching it back. "I'll take that, punk."

Russo and Ahmed gathered their things and started to leave the cockpit while Timmons returned the Brain to the protective case.

Russo turned back. "I gotta go enter the logbook page in the computer. You gonna sign the Brain Kit back in to the parts department?"

"Yeah, yeah, get outta here. I got it." Timmons waved them away. "And I ain't paying you no money; the game was rigged." Pointing to Ahmed, he said, his voice dripping with jealousy, "Why don't you try hitting up trust fund baby here for the money?"

Ahmed's dark eyes narrowed as he thrust his finger in his tormenter's face. "Screw you, Timmons! I don't want any of my dad's tainted, capitalist pig money."

Seeing he had gotten under Ahmed's skin, Timmons gladly turned the knife. "Funny, that don't stop you from driving Daddy's Porsche, though. Friggin' ingrate."

Russo stepped between the two men before they came to blows. "Don't pay no attention to him, Ahmed. He's just jealous." As he ushered Ahmed out of the cockpit, Russo turned, raised his middle finger, and gave Timmons the New York salute. "Ya big loooser!"

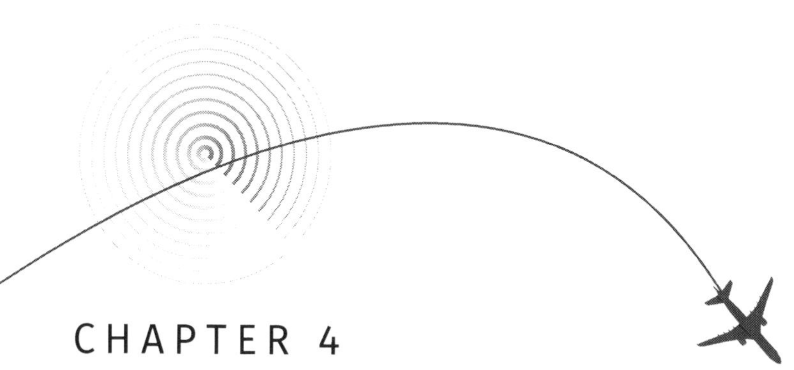

CHAPTER 4

MARK WALKED ALONE, eyes cast downward, down a long hallway on an upper floor in the hangar. It was brightly lit by harsh fluorescent lights hanging under rusting metal hoods. His heels clacked and echoed as he walked across the faded and cracked linoleum tile. Mark lugged a well-traveled sky-blue Samsonite suitcase in one hand and a worn black leather flight bag in the other.

The fresh coat of tan paint on the cinderblock walls wasn't fooling anyone. Like most hangars at JFK, it had been around since the field was originally called Idlewild Airport. The old hangar had a well-known reputation in the airline industry of being cursed after serving as the home of two previous airlines that went belly up. Alpha

Airline's precarious financial condition, as it struggled to become profitable, was close to adding another casualty to the list.

Mark stopped at a door with a black plastic sign labeled FLIGHT PLANNING jutting out from the wall.

The large room had plate glass windows on the far side that overlooked the hangar floor below. A row of computers on the opposite wall sat ready for use by flight crews. Yellowing paper aviation maps were pinned to cork bulletin boards around the room. They displayed routes to various parts of the globe using a language only a pilot could decipher. A large table, used to spread out maps and plan routes, occupied the middle of the room.

Two pilots, with three gold stripes at the end of their jacket sleeves, were engaged in a weighty conversation. Mohammad Aziz, a small, wiry man with dark eyes and a full head of dark hair, had his hand outstretched. "Okay, it's agreed then?" he said quietly, with an anxious look on his face.

Walter Barns, a young guy wearing thick glasses, who obviously hadn't missed too many meals, hesitated. He looked at the floor. Walter contemplated the important question posed to him by Mohammad. Out of nervous habit, he pushed his glasses back up the bridge of his nose. Walter looked up and reluctantly shook Mohammad's hand. "All right, Mo. I better not be sorry."

"Trust me," Mo assured.

Unaware they were being watched, the two pilots heard, "Hey guys." They turned to see Mark standing in the doorway. He didn't recognize either of the pilots—not uncommon when working at a major airline that employed thousands of them. Mark walked up to the pair. "You guys working the London flight with me on the Tech-Liner?"

Mo nodded. "That's us."

Mark shook their hands. "I'm Mark Smith."

Mohammad reached out. "Mo, the relief pilot."

Walter did the same. "Nice to meet you, Captain Smith. I'm Walter Barns. I'll be your copilot."

Mark thought, *these damned copilots look younger every day. They barely look old enough to drive, let alone fly airliners. Is this the flight planning room or a day care center?*

During mandatory, touchy-feely Captain Leadership Training it was "suggested" to captains that they try to develop rapport early when working with a new crew by taking a personal interest in their copilots. Mark asked the men the industry standard question. "You guys live locally?"

"Florida," Mo responded.

"We both commute out of Miami. Long flight to the JFK base but sure beats the weather here."

"And the taxes," Mo tossed in.

Enough with the small talk. Mark asked, "You print out the flight paperwork yet?"

"Nope!"

Mo proudly held up an iPad, tapping on the screen. "It's all in here: flight plan, approach charts, manuals, everything. No more Dark Ages."

"Here's yours, Captain." Walter slid a tablet over to Mark.

He looked down at it dismissively. "Damned gadgets. Great, until they fail, of course. Then what?"

Walter cheerfully held up his iPad. "That's why we have three."

Mark pushed the tablet away like it was a rotting fish. "I don't want that damned thing." Patting the left breast of his jacket, he said, "I've got the most high-tech tool ever invented right here."

Mo and Walter looked intrigued.

Mark continued. "Never needs charging. Never crashes. Never needs Wi-Fi." He reached into the inside pocket of his uniform jacket and pulled it out.

"It's called a pen."

Not done yet, Mark's sarcastic side emerged. "You use it on this..." He held up a map then laid it out on the large table. "Pilots call this a map. Maybe you whiz kids have heard of them?"

Ever the smart ass, Mo quipped, "A map? How do you spell that? I'll Google it."

Mark shot him a sideways glance. *Damned Millennials, no respect.* He longed for the old days when copilots facetiously referred to their captains as "sky gods." He glared at Mo then asked, "Everything else done, Walter?"

Smart enough not to test Mark's patience any further, Walter responded, "Everything checks out okay, sir. The flight plan has been filed. I downloaded the route directly into the cockpit computers. No need to enter it manually. Fuel's good."

"Any room for a little more?" Mark asked.

"We're about seven thousand pounds under max takeoff weight. Could fill it up if you want," Walter volunteered.

Having been around the block more than once, Mark knew the benefits of having extra fuel on board. He educated his young copilots. "Boys, the only time your plane can have too much fuel is when it's on fire." Mark walked over to a side door in the room labeled DISPATCH. Not so much asking as telling, Mark said, "Hey, Bill, top off the Tech-Liner, will ya," then chuckled, "put it on my tab."

Bill, the dispatcher assigned to the London flight, looked up from his computer work station. Seeing his old friend, Bill grinned broadly as he broke the bad news. "Sorry, Mark, your credit is no good here. No can do. Last-minute cargo just added. You'll have to live with what you got."

According to FAA regulations, airline dispatchers had as much say over what happens with a flight as the pilots. Captains had no choice other than to accept this emasculating arrangement. If being honest, though, they were more than happy to let the dispatchers do all the grunt work of manually planning long, complicated international flights.

"Who the hell made that boneheaded decision?" Mark angrily asked Bill.

"I did, Smith."

Mark wheeled around to see Mike Andrews lurking in the doorway, glaring at him with contempt in his beady eyes.

"What do you mean *you* did? I'm the captain on this flight!"

Andrews puffed out his chest. "And I'm the CEO of this airline. I'm not your copilot anymore, Smith, get used to it. The fuel meets the FAA minimum requirement. End of discussion."

Mark wasn't about to let his authority be usurped that easily, especially in front of his copilots. "What cargo is so damn precious that fuel is—"

"One of our VIP passengers decided to bring his Rolls Royce with him to London."

"A car? Over fuel? Are you kidding me?" Mo was incredulous.

Feeling it was beneath him to justify his decision to a mere copilot, Andrews ignored Mo. "I told him we'd be happy to accommodate his request. I'm charging him an extra three thousand to haul it. That's what's known in the airline management world as a savvy business decision, gentlemen. Something you jet jockeys have obviously never heard of. We take off in forty-five minutes. Be ready." With that last jab, Andrews strutted out of the room.

Mo looked at Mark in disbelief. "*He* used to be a pilot?"

Mark nodded.

Mo couldn't hold his tongue any longer. "Weasel!"

Mark's cell phone rang. He fished out an old-style Motorola flip phone from his pocket. "Hello? Oh, hey sweetie, what's up?"

MARY SMITH WAS leaning back on a mound of pillows on her dorm room bed wearing only a Duke University T-shirt and panties. Cute, rebellious, and an only child, she was used to getting her way. Her boyfriend, Randy, who was definitely not "Dad approved," slouched nearby smoking a joint. She whined into her dorm room phone, "Dad, the registrar's office called and said they still haven't received the tuition check for this semester. I thought you were going to take care of it."

Mark winced. "Ah crap, I forgot. When do you need it by?"

Let down by her father once again, Mary implored, "Dad! It has to be paid by the end of this week! They said if it's late again they're going to kick me out of school!"

Mark tried to calm her down. "OK, relax, I'll take care of it."

"Promise?"

"I'm leaving tonight for London. I'll send the check as soon as I get back. Promise." Mark shouldn't have asked but couldn't help himself. "I don't suppose your mother is going to help out with tuition?"

Mary protested, "Dad, you know I don't like it when you guys put me in the middle like that. Can we not do this right now?"

Mark immediately regretted his words. "I know, I know. Sorry." Apprehensively, he said, "I've been meaning to tell you something. This is my last trip. I'm retiring."

Silence.

Mark wasn't sure she heard him. "Mary?"

"I heard you, Dad. What do you expect me to say?"

Mark reached out to his only daughter. "I was hoping you would...I was hoping now that I'll have more free time we could..."

"You're not really going to say it, are you?"

"It?"

"That whole father-daughter bonding line again."

"Something like that."

Mary's eyes misted up. "Father? Daughter? My whole childhood you were always flying. I barely saw you. And when I did, you were drunk."

Ouch!

Mark resisted the urge to make excuses for his past behavior. He tried to redeem himself. "Look, I admit I wasn't always the best father. But I'm trying to change that. I'm trying to make things right with you and me. If you would just give me a chance..."

"Now that I'm swamped with medical school you *finally* have time for me?"

Oblivious to the deep-seated pain she was feeling, her boyfriend waved away a cloud of smoke and offered her a toke. Mary angrily pushed him away. Randy slouched back down into the chair.

"I'm not asking for much of your time. I know you're busy."

"I've got to go to class. Maybe we can talk about this later. I really gotta go." She slammed the phone down. Tears, representing years of pain, gushed out.

THE LOUD CLICK rang in Mark's ear like a slamming door.

He looked up from the phone and saw both his copilots staring directly at him. They immediately averted their eyes downward, suddenly interested in their shoes.

Mark looked back down and said, unconvincingly, "OK, sweetie, I'll talk to you later." He waited three seconds then said, "I love you, too." Mark slid the flip phone back into his pocket.

Awkward silence filled the room.

Walter finally spoke. "Sooo...Retiring, huh? What are you going to do with yourself?"

"Hell if I know. Whatever irrelevant old fossils do when they're forced out to pasture."

Walter tried to cheer up Mark. "Hey, Mo. You know what we ought to do? We ought to throw Mark a retirement party when we get to London."

Mo grinned. "Damn right, we should. After this trip is over, we move up one number on the seniority list."

Mark shook his head. "Great. My last trip, and I get paired up with Laurel and Hardy." He picked up his suitcase, flight bag, and map and walked out.

Looking puzzled, Walter turned to Mo. "Who?"

Mo just shrugged his shoulders.

CHAPTER 5

SEVEN FLIGHT ATTENDANTS were loosely gathered in the front of the Tech-Liner cabin. They gossiped and texted simultaneously before the passengers boarded the plane. One admired herself in a compact mirror, adding yet another layer to her makeup.

Noelle Parker stood out among the group with her fiery red hair and piercing crystal-blue eyes. She was one of the lucky few to win the genetic lottery. With a willowy body, poised demeanor, and stunning good looks, Noelle's time as a model in her younger days was still readily apparent, even at fifty. Women decades her junior were envious.

Although tired of the never-ending craziness that plagued the airline industry, Noelle still enjoyed the perks of being a flight attendant. A boring office job, stuck in a cube farm all day, would never have afforded her the same amount of time off. And certainly not the free travel to interesting destinations on those days off. The low pay was a different matter. Graduating as her high school class valedictorian, Noelle had been savvy enough to stash away most of the money she made in Paris the next three years as a high-fashion model—working a different type of runway. Enough money to get a degree at Yale. After graduating magna cum laude with a BA in French, at the ancient age of twenty-five, modeling was no longer an option. Being the free spirit in the family, she decided to pass on joining the family business and pursue the "glamorous," if not lucrative, life of a flight attendant.

As is often the case, that free-spirited personality, combined with her beauty, had attracted the wrong kind of men in her quest for love. Despite the calluses that had built up around her heart over the years, she was still a romantic. Noelle held out a glimmer of hope of someday finding her one true soul mate. But trusting men was very difficult for her after all the hurt she had experienced.

Noelle was busy catching up on the latest with her best friend, Charlotte. Flight attendants like Charlotte, with many, many decades of seniority, were known among crews as "Senior Mammas"—big, bitchy, and bossy. Although her coworkers wouldn't dare call her that to her face, Charlotte had certainly earned the nickname. Originally a genteel Southern belle from Atlanta, it had been a long time since she'd won any congeniality contests. As the most senior stew in the crew, Charlotte relished her role as the enforcer when passengers got out of hand.

"Sorry to hear about Bubba's accident. How's he handling crutches?" Noelle said to her friend.

"Ornery as hell," Charlotte grumbled. "He's worse than a damned passenger. 'Git me this. Fetch me that.' If he ain't careful, I'm fixin' to give him a new reason to visit the hospital."

Noelle shook her head. "Men. They're all the same. He better not tangle with you, that's all I have to say." Noelle gestured to the group, "Okay, let's get started."

"Hush, y'all. The purser wants to brief us!" Charlotte barked. They immediately quieted down as Charlotte commanded.

Thankful to have a seasoned crew to work with on this important trip, Noelle started her preflight briefing. "Good evening, everyone. I've worked with most of you in the past, so I'll keep the briefing short. We have a special first-class configuration throughout the aircraft for tonight's inaugural flight. Our passengers include VIPs, invited guests, and first-flight contest winners. Please don't hesitate to come to me if you have any problems during the flight. Our captain tonight is..." She shuffled through her paperwork looking for the names of tonight's pilots. Noelle shook her head ever so slightly. A frown crossed her face. "Mark Smith." Noelle and Charlotte exchanged a knowing look. "He'll have our flight time when he gets here. Any questions for me right now?" There weren't. "OK, thank you, everyone."

MARK LUGGED HIS Samsonite and flight bag across the hangar floor toward the boarding stairs. His copilots strode single file behind him, leisurely wheeling their suitcases. The three pilots ascended the stairs and walked into the forward part of the cabin. Mo and Walter admired the posh surroundings, checked out the flight attendants, then headed for the cockpit to start their preflight duties. Mark looked around wistfully at the impressive machine that was taking him to London. Out of habit, he patted the door frame like an old friend then let out a deep sigh. "My last trip. All right, let's get this over with." He walked up to the flight attendants. "Good evening, everyone. I'm Mark Smith. I'll be your..."

Noelle turned around, arms defiantly crossed, and faced Mark.

Surprised to see Noelle, Mark did his best to hide it. He cleared his throat then continued. "I'll be your captain for tonight's flight. Ms. Parker, I see you are going to be the purser."

"You see correctly, Captain Smith." Gesturing to her left, Noelle said, "My *trustworthy* friend, Charlotte, will be the assistant purser."

Great, here we go again, Mark thought.

Mark barely glanced her way and nodded. "Charlotte."

Charlotte shot daggers with her eyes. "Captain Smith."

The tension hanging in the air was broken when Tina Reynolds, a buxom platinum blonde who purposefully wore her uniform one size too small, bounced up to Mark. She extended her right hand, decked out with sparkling costume jewelry, and purred, "Captain Mark, it's a pleasure to meet you. I'm Tina."

Mark shook Tina's hand, trying not to ogle too long at her ample, well-advertised cleavage. He continued. "Our takeoff time is during rush hour for international departures, so expect about a forty-five-minute taxi. Once we get airborne, our flight time tonight will be seven and a half hours. The standard security measures everyone is aware of are in place. Weather on our route tonight is..." Mark looked up and saw one of the flight attendants ignoring him, texting on her phone.

He stopped and stared at her.

She didn't notice.

All the flight attendants glared at her.

She *still* didn't notice.

Mark's patience quickly ran out. He loudly cleared his throat. The flight attendant finally looked up. Red faced, she put away her phone.

"As I was saying, the weather on our route tonight is not the best. Expect some light to moderate turbulence. I'm sure I don't have to tell you how important this trip is to our company."

Noelle jumped in. "You're right, you don't. Trust me, my team and I will do everything possible to make sure the trip goes smoothly. This isn't my first rodeo."

Under his breath, Mark said to himself, "Obviously." With a forced smile, he looked up and grudgingly said, "I'm sure you will, Ms. Parker. I look forward to working with...with all of you."

Noelle asserted her authority, at least in the confines of the passenger cabin. "We need to get ready for boarding. Will there be anything else, Captain?"

"No, Ms. Parker, apparently not." Mark turned and walked away. When out of earshot of the group he muttered, "Well, this should be fun."

"*Okay*, no tension there," Tina said sarcastically. "Reminds me of me and my exes."

Noelle and Charlotte shook their heads.

Tina hadn't picked up on the situation yet. "What?"

Charlotte finally spelled it out. "He's her ex."

The light bulb, dim as it may have been, finally came on. "Oooohh...Oh, I see." The gold digger in Tina didn't take long to come out. "So...that means he's available then...right, Noelle?"

Noelle clenched her jaw and glared at Tina. She felt an unexpected twinge of jealousy. *Wait...why should I care if some bimbo wants to ruin Mark's life? Serves him right. It's not like I care about him anymore.*

Charlotte came to the aid of her friend. "Honey, he must be twice your age."

Tina glowered at Charlotte. "That's no problem. So were all my exes, *honey*!" Tina marched off to the back of the plane.

CHAPTER 6

FLIGHT ALPHA ONE was not a scheduled commercial flight available to the hoi polloi. Its passengers would be boarding their flight directly from inside the hangar. They were thankful to avoid the sea of humanity and typical pandemonium that plagued JFK Terminal 4. To satisfy the TSA, the passengers funneled through a makeshift security screening checkpoint set up on the hangar floor. It consisted of one security guard with a metal detection wand.

The eclectic group included: Russians, Chinese, Saudis in white robes (followed by women covered head to toe), tech titans, business people, assorted Europeans, aviation nuts who enter first-flight contests, and even a few Canadians.

High maintenance was an understatement.

J. Alexander Hampton, sixty-four, with perfectly coiffed gray hair, was Alpha Airlines chairman of the board. A Harvard Business School alumni pin held a prominent place on the lapel of his bespoke Ermenegildo Zegna suit. He worked the line, glad-handing each VIP passenger. "Welcome, thanks for coming. I'm so glad you're here."

Hampton frowned and looked down, trying to avoid interacting with the next passenger in line. He didn't succeed. François Laurent, a tall, aloof, ascot-wearing Frenchman, reached out and vigorously shook Hampton's hand. "Alexander, mon ami! How nice to see you." Dripping with insincerity, Laurent said, "It was thoughtful of you to invite me on the inaugural flight."

Hampton had no choice but to stop. "It was the least we could do, François, after you and Airbus worked so hard to try to win our aircraft order. Sorry it didn't work out."

On Laurent's left was a small, wiry Chinese man in his mid-thirties. The man's round glasses surrounded intense, angry eyes. Laurent gestured toward him. "Alexander, let me introduce our head of IT, Dr. Lu Wong. He is the mastermind behind the groundbreaking computer network on our new plane."

Hampton extended his hand. "Nice to meet you, Doctor." Wong glared at Hampton, leaving his arms frozen at his side.

Laurent jumped in to apologize. "You'll have to excuse Dr. Wong. He feels his technology is far superior to the Tech-Liner's. It's nothing personal, of course."

"No, of course not," Hampton sniffed.

Not willing to let a seven-billion-dollar order slip away, Laurent said, "As the VP of sales, I'm obliged to let you know, my good friend, it's not too late to reconsider. After today's flight I predict you'll want to rethink the risky bet your CEO has made on this unproven plane." Laurent gestured toward the striking twenty-four-year-old blonde woman next to him. "I'll have my executive assistant send you and the board a completely revised contract the moment we land." She chomped on a wad of gum, eyes glued to her iPhone, as the two men leered longer than appropriate at her sheer white blouse tucked into a skintight leopard-print skirt.

Hampton snapped, "The board fully supports our CEO's decision, François. Enjoy the flight." He started to walk away then stopped, looking the perky aerobics instructor turned "assistant" up and down. Turning back to Laurent, Hampton said, "Give my best to your wife."

Behind the philandering Frenchman in line was Jan Frey. Her pearls, chic Dior outfit, and Manolo Blahnik heels didn't quite camouflage the hectic reality of trying to balance motherhood, marriage, and career. Jan was busy checking her work emails on one device and talking into another held in place between her tilted head and left shoulder. "Tommy's mother will pick you guys up after school and take you to your game. I know, I know, I wish I could go to your game too, sweetie. I'll be back in just a few days. Please remind your sister to clean her room." Jan listened for a moment then her smile evaporated. "No, no, that's okay. Don't tell him I'm on the phone. I'll say hi to Daddy when I get home. Love you. Bye, bye." Jan had something in her eye she wiped away with a Kleenex.

Hampton walked up to Hernandez and eagerly shook his hand. "Administrator Hernandez, so glad you could join us."

Hernandez responded tepidly. "My pleasure, Alexander, looking forward to it." He nervously looked down at his watch. Hernandez's government-issue Blackberry rang. HOME was displayed on the caller ID. He answered. "Administrator Hernandez. What? When? Have you notified my team?" A look of concern flashed across his face. "I'll be on the next flight back to DC."

"Is there a problem, Michael?" Hampton asked.

"An urgent matter has come up back at my office. I'm afraid I won't be able to go on the flight, Alexander. Duty calls."

"I completely understand. Maybe some other time," Hampton said with a weak smile.

Hernandez scurried off toward the nearest exit.

J. Alexander Hampton walked to the front of the line, cut in front of the passengers, and climbed the stairs to board the plane.

CHAPTER 7

THE PASSENGERS SLOWLY shuffled on board the plane. They marveled at the opulent interior in their native tongues. Charlotte greeted each one in her native tongue. "Welcome aboard our flight this evening, y'all."

The large Saudi entourage entered the plane. Prince Omar bin Basara, owner of Air Saudi Airlines and wealthy member of the royal family, led the group. He was wearing the traditional white thawb garment and sported a large beard—and an even larger waistline.

Charlotte enthusiastically greeted him. "Prince Basara, we're honored to have you on board with us." He completely ignored her and walked off. Charlotte was stunned at the rude treatment.

A veiled Saudi woman in the group apologized. "The prince wishes to say he is honored to be here as well."

Charlotte muttered to herself. "I think someone is a little too big for his britches." Going back to her duties, she picked up the PA microphone and announced, "On behalf of Alpha Airlines, I'd like to welcome y'all on board our beautiful new Tech-Liner for its inaugural flight to London. In honor of this special occasion, you'll find laptops provided at every seat, complimentary satellite internet service, HD screens for your viewing pleasure, lay-flat seats, and during the flight, a seven-course gourmet dinner."

The Frenchman Laurent turned back toward Charlotte with an incredulous look on his face. "Airline food? Gourmet? Sacre bleu!"

Passengers settled in their seats, wasting no time diving in to their Tumi amenity kits stuffed with luxurious toiletries to pamper themselves with during the long flight.

MO, WALTER, AND Mark were in the cockpit, busy getting the plane ready for their flight. Mo tapped Walter on the arm. "Did you see the blonde flight attendant when we got on? Cute."

Walter did notice. "Nice rack, too. What do you think, Mark? Not bad, huh?"

Mark looked at his copilots and shook his head. He could have wasted his time trying to warn them about the complications that come with getting involved with flight attendants, but he would obviously have been hypocritical. Besides, the young guys never listened anyways. “I need some coffee. You guys want anything?”

“No, I’m good,” Walter replied.

With an appalled look on his face, Mo said, “American coffee?! I’ll pass.”

“Suit yourself,” Mark said as he walked out of the cockpit.

NOELLE BUSILY PREPARED the forward galley before takeoff. Upset about the unexpected pairing with her ex, she slammed door after door, taking her anger out on the defenseless metal cabinets lining the galley.

“Is it safe to get a cup of coffee?” Mark said as he hesitantly entered the galley.

She refused to look up, pointing to the coffee machine.

It would have taken a logging chainsaw to cut the tension in the air.

Mark grabbed the stainless-steel coffee pot from the coffeemaker and poured himself a cup. Leaning against the counter, he tested the temperature with a small, cautious sip. Despite the bitter aftertaste, Mark decided it was safe to try more. After a few more sips, he volunteered, "Just so you know, I was assigned this trip. I didn't ask for it."

No response from Noelle.

Another small sip. "What say we pretend to get along for the next few days, okay? This is my last trip, and I just want it to go smoothly."

Noelle finally looked up. "You're retiring?"

"According to the geniuses at the FAA, next week I won't be safe to fly airliners anymore."

Noelle winced inside at forgetting his birthday was coming up. Feigning disinterest, she probed, "Any plans?"

"I'm not sure yet. I got an offer to fly cargo out of Cincinnati. I'll probably go do that for a while. Beats sitting in my dreary apartment watching reruns."

Noelle couldn't help but give her two cents. "Flying boxes back and forth all night? You'd hate that."

"At least boxes won't criticize me if I make a bad landing."

Noelle ignored the jab. "There's more to life than flying airplanes, Mark. Get out of this rat race. Do something fun for once. Buy a boat. Sail the world. Enjoy your life."

Mark sensed a slightly encouraging change in Noelle's tone. *No, I'm probably reading too much into it*, he thought. Mark replied, "A boat? Me? You know the reason that's not going to happen."

Noelle hinted, "You know...Mary could use a father figure in her life right now."

"She doesn't want to have anything to do with me."

"Can you blame her?"

Mark sighed. "My whole life, I swore I would never turn out like my old man: a divorced alcoholic whose kid hated him. Now look at me. I guess they're right. The apple doesn't fall far from the tree." Mark forced the bitter memories from his mind as quickly as they had appeared. "At least I'm good for something—tuition." He tested the waters. "I don't suppose you're going to pitch in, are you?"

"You know I can't afford medical school tuition, Mark."

Mark fired back. "Well, Dan sure as hell can."

Sadness washed over Noelle's face. She said softly, "If you must know, I kicked him out months ago. Turns out he's not the only cheating pilot out there."

Proving he didn't understand women very well, instead of being sympathetic, Mark unwisely added, "See, I was right. You should have listened to me. I warned you about him."

Noelle snapped, "Well you should know, shouldn't you?" As soon as the words left Noelle's mouth she regretted them. "I'm sorry. I shouldn't have said that."

"Can't honestly say I don't deserve it. I know you don't believe me, but I've changed."

She turned her head to prevent Mark from seeing tears welling up in her pretty blue eyes. "Please, how many times have I heard *that* before? Look, I don't want to fight with you, Mark. Let's just pretend to get along."

Trying to cheer his ex-wife up, and perhaps holding out a little hope at mending their fractured relationship, Mark said, "Sorry about you and Dan. I mean that. How about this? During the layover we go to your favorite place for dinner and talk. Just you and me."

Noelle gave thought to accepting Mark's offer when Tina suddenly popped into the galley. "Oh, there you are, Mark. I've been looking all over for you." She looked at Noelle, then back to Mark. "I see you're available."

Noelle quickly wiped away her tear then turned around. "What is it, Ms. Reynolds?"

"A passenger has an issue. He—"

"Tell the passenger I'll be back in a minute to talk to him."

"His wife said he will only speak to the captain."

"Tell him—"

Mark stepped in. "It's okay, Noelle, I'll take care of it."

Tina gloated. "Thank you, Captain Mark. Please, come with me." She hooked her arm around Mark's. Tina flashed a triumphant smirk back at Noelle, then led him away.

Noelle glared at Tina as she walked away cozying up next to her husband. Correction, ex-husband.

Another defenseless cabinet door felt Noelle's wrath.

✈

MARK AND TINA walked down the aisle, maneuvering around a passenger trying to jam his oversize bag into the overhead bin. Mark shook his head. *There's always that one passenger who drags a bag on the plane the size of a steamer trunk, positive they will find some novel way to shoehorn it into the bin.*

As they walked up to the Saudi entourage, Basara handed his outer garment to one of his wives. He dismissively waved her away with a flick of his wrist.

Tina introduced Mark. "Prince Basara, this is Captain—"

Incensed that a woman would dare speak to him, Basara held up his hand like a stop sign, commanding her to stop.

"Excuse me?!" Tina snapped.

He looked condescendingly at Mark. "*Captain*, I see my Rolls Royce is about to be loaded." Basara pointed out the aircraft window to the hangar floor.

The $450,000 silver Rolls Royce Ghost was carefully strapped down on a metal cargo pallet. Four-inch-wide braided nylon straps, padded underneath with sheepskin, crisscrossed the hood, the trunk, and along the length of the car front to back. No metal chains were allowed to touch His Royal Highness's pride and joy. Cargo personnel were busy getting it ready to load into the belly of the plane.

Basara continued. "I demand that it is loaded last. I don't want your laborers to scratch it."

So, this is the passenger that kept me from getting all the gas I wanted. Mark tried to be diplomatic. "I'm sure your car will be—"

"Rolls Royce."

Mark gritted his teeth. "I'm sure your *Rolls Royce* will be just fine. Our people are very careful."

Andrews was lurking nearby, eavesdropping. He interjected, "Prince Basara, allow me to introduce myself. I'm Mike Andrews, CEO of Alpha Airlines. I will see to it personally your Rolls Royce is handled with kid gloves and loaded last. You have my personal guarantee it won't have a scratch on it."

"Thank you, Mr....?"

"Andrews. But please, call me Mike."

Mark shook his head. *It's getting deep in here.* He was more than happy to let Andrews deal with the entitled Basara. "If you gentlemen will excuse me, I have some *important* duties to attend to."

Mark made his way back to the cockpit, avoiding the forward galley.

CHAPTER 8

MARK ENTERED THE cockpit—his second home. The place he dreamed of ending up as a kid. The place he'd spent, if all his flight hours were added up, almost two continuous years in. The place that also cost him his family.

After neatly hanging up his uniform jacket in the coat closet, Mark slid comfortably into the captain's seat. He asked Walter, who was sitting in the right seat, "Everything done?"

"All set, Captain."

"Let's go to London." Mark grabbed the hand microphone and punched the intercom button on the radio panel to speak to the mechanic down below. "Tug. Cockpit. You there?"

A diesel tug sprouted a long tow bar connected at the other end to the nose gear of the plane. The tug looked like a massive block of steel with tires at each corner. Only a machine with its mass and ridiculously low gearing could pull the nearly one million pounds the fully loaded plane weighed. The portly tug driver pushed his headset boom mic up to his lips. "I'm down here. You flyboys all set up there?"

Mark never cared for that nickname for pilots. But at this point in his career, what would be the point of complaining. "Cockpit's ready."

"Close her up," the driver said.

Mark tapped a red door symbol on the center cockpit screen labeled AFT CARGO DOOR. On the right side of the plane, behind the wing, the 10'x10' curved cargo door slowly arced downward, pulled by two thick silver rods attached to either side. The rods slowly receded into their hydraulic actuators until the door was flush with the fuselage. The symbol on the screen turned green.

Mark informed the tug driver. "The aft cargo door is closed and locked. It's all yours."

A red light on the bottom of the fuselage began to flash. It was the universal warning signal to anyone nearby that the plane was about to move.

The segmented hangar doors slowly parted while the tug driver revved up the powerful diesel engine. A thick black cloud spewed from the exhaust pipe. Fourteen nitrogen-filled Goodyear Aviation tires, taller than the average man, grudgingly rolled forward off their flat spots. At a walking pace, the tug pulled the behemoth out onto the ramp. The world's newest commercial airliner was brought out of the warm, safe hangar into the cold, cruel world for the first time as just another revenue-generating asset.

THE TECH-LINER WAS equipped with a wide-angle camera mounted at the top of its tail. It gave the pilots a bird's-eye view of their plane and the area ahead of it. Considering the cockpit was thirty feet above the ground and perched behind a huge, bulbous nose cone, the view from the camera was a godsend for flight crews. Walter pulled up the feed from the tail camera on the center cockpit screen. He carefully scanned it, looking for any obstacles or FOD (debris that could get sucked into the engines) the driver might not see as he maneuvered the tug in reverse.

Before cranking up the engines, Mark rattled off his standard welcome aboard speech to the passengers. After delivering the same spiel hundreds of times, it was no wonder the greeting sounded unenthusiastic.

IN THE CABIN, the mind-numbing safety information video played. It featured a cast of perky airline employees—or more accurately, aspiring actors auditioning their talents and hoping to be discovered. Thankfully, after five minutes explaining how to unbuckle a seatbelt, it came to an end. Noelle walked slowly down the aisle checking on her passengers. A frowning Russian had his laptop open, tapping away. He looked like the stereotypical ill-tempered Cold War villain from central casting: an ox-like build, a broad Slavic face, thick neck, dark hair, and ruddy complexion. The color that came from consuming copious amounts of Vodka to endure long Russian winters.

Noelle advised him, "Sir, you'll have to stow your laptop until we get above ten thousand feet."

The Russian looked up, bared his tobacco-stained teeth, and brusquely replied, "As you wish." Then he said something in Russian that probably didn't translate to the same phrase.

Charlotte walked up to report the status of the cabin. "We're all set for takeoff, Noelle. Ten crew, one hundred pax" (industry slang for passengers).

Noelle picked up the handset at the front flight attendant panel and pressed the button labeled COCKPIT. She reported, "Cabin's ready, Captain."

Mark replied, "Thanks, Noelle. We're number fourteen in line for takeoff. Think about my offer in London, okay?"

Caught off guard by the invitation, Noelle hung up without answering. She held on to the handset and pondered the offer for a moment. *What could be the harm in meeting Mark for an innocent dinner? Grab a quick bite. Call it a night. End of story. Besides, someone needs to warn Mark about that snake Tina.*

Charlotte interrupted her train of thought. "So, your favorite place for dinner in London?"

Noelle looked surprised. "What?"

"You. Me. Wellington Pub. What did you think I meant?"

"Right. Wellington Pub. Uh...do you mind terribly if I take a rain check?"

"But you love their food." Suspicious as to why her friend would pass up the best fish and chips in London, Charlotte gave her a disapproving look.

Noelle tried to hide her inner thoughts from her long-time friend. "What? Can't a person have some time alone?"

"You're not thinking about spending the layover with *him*, are you?"

"No, of course not. No. I'm just not feeling well, that's all."

Charlotte choose not to call her friend out on her fib. "Okay, honey, maybe next time." She winked, "You take care of those *feelings* of yours, ya hear."

"Thanks for understanding, Charlotte. You're the best."

"You let me know if you change your mind."

Noelle sat down on the jumpseat attached to the front wall of the cabin, next to the door. She looked out at the planeload of eager faces excited to start their journey. The thought crossed her mind, *how many thousands of passengers have I served over my career? Taken care of their every need. What about me? Who'll take care of me one day when I'm older?* Noelle picked up the PA mic and forced an obligatory smile. "We are ready for takeoff, so please sit back, relax, and enjoy the inaugural flight of Alpha Airlines new Tech-Liner."

AFTER INCHING ALONG in an aluminum conga line of airliners for forty-five minutes, Mark finally taxied the plane up to the hold short line at the north end of the runway. Storm clouds could be seen building to the east.

Walter radioed the tower, "JFK tower, Alpha One ready for takeoff."

In the terse, rapid-fire language of air traffic control, the tower responded, "Alpha One cleared for takeoff on runway two two right. On departure turn left to zero-nine-zero degrees. Climb to niner thousand."

As trained, Walter repeated back the instructions exactly as given. The verbatim readback was designed to prevent a fatal miscommunication as the plane threaded its way through the most congested airspace on earth.

Mark lined up the plane on the white painted stripes running down the centerline of the runway. "Select takeoff mode," he ordered.

Walter pressed a button on the keypad built in to the center console. The throttles moved full forward by themselves. The low-throated whine of the two turbofan engines rapidly built to a deafening roar. Four million cubic feet of air per minute were ravenously ingested by the low-hanging engines. Loose snow was sucked up off the runway as if by a gigantic vacuum cleaner.

Despite being laden with hundreds of thousands of pounds of fuel inside the wings, the tips slowly rose, flexing the long metal lifting surfaces until they supported the weight of the plane. When the Tech-Liner reached the takeoff speed automatically determined by the computer, Walter called out, "Vee-One. Rotate," meaning there was no going back now.

Mark gently pulled back on his control stick. With only a few ounces of effort on his part, the metal behemoth raised its nose toward the heavens and lumbered off the runway. Swirls of snow were violently kicked up by two hundred and fifty thousand pounds of combined thrust as the plane climbed up into the black night sky. After hand-flying for a few miles, Mark happily let the autopilot—"George"—take it from there.

An hour and a half later the plane crossed into Canadian airspace. Walter keyed his mic. "Gander Oceanic, Alpha One entering your airspace. Level at thirty-five thousand feet."

Gander Oceanic was the name of the Nav Canada ATC (Air Traffic Control) facility responsible for controlling aircraft in the oceanic airspace east of Canada. In a dark, smoke-filled room, the perpetually stressed out, chain-smoking controller responded, "Alpha One, radar contact. Proceed as filed on North Atlantic Track Quebec."

"Roger. Alpha One is cleared as filed on to NAT track Quebec."

IN THE CABIN, flight attendants began serving dinner. The Russian waved his empty glass at Charlotte. "Stewardess, another vodka."

She walked over to his seat for the fifth time. "Sir, don't you think you oughta have some supper before having any more to drink?"

Slurring his words, he said, "You call that slop food? In my country we call it gruel!" He let out a hearty laugh at Charlotte's expense.

Charlotte planted her fists on her hips and glared at the inebriated Slav. In a thick Southern drawl, Charlotte said, "Gruel? Well, bless your little heart, Ivan. You know what we call fellas like you in my country? We call 'em—"

Noelle stepped in, just in the nick of time. "I've got this, Charlotte. Why don't you see if the gals in the back need any help?"

Charlotte huffed at the Russian, then stomped off.

THE PILOTS HAD removed their headsets and listened for calls from ATC on the cockpit speaker. Gander Oceanic called. "Alpha One you are leaving radio and radar coverage. Cleared to switch to autonomous satellite communications and navigation. If you need to contact Gander Oceanic, send a CPDLC data-link text message via SatComm. Contact Shannon ATC on voice when you reach the other side. Have a safe trip."

"Roger Gander, switching to autonomous. Alpha One out," Walter replied on the hand mic.

"Finally, some peace and quiet," Mo whined.

"Going autonomous," Mark said. He waited for any objections from his copilots, then pressed a button on the keypad. The pilots could now sit back and relax while crossing the pond as the plane did all the work.

Mark settled in for hours of monotony until they arrived at the east side of the Atlantic. He leaned back and took a long sip of coffee. Without much else to do, Mark peered out his side window. Above the northern horizon, shimmering curtains of azure and emerald-green light from the aurora borealis swayed back and forth as if in a trance. Mark had traveled the world, but nothing could match the strange beauty of this otherworldly light show when viewed from the heavens. He looked down, noting the stark contrast between the beautiful colors of the aurora and the dark ocean below. The light from the moon cast a silvery reflection off the water. City-block-size icebergs dotted the surface. An occasional pinpoint of light highlighted the location of a lone fishing boat trying to scratch out a living.

A LARGE VIDEO screen on the front wall of the cabin displayed a map spanning the Atlantic Ocean. A curved white line depicted tonight's planned route to London. The plane's current location east of the Canadian mainland was marked with a tiny airplane icon. The airliner would be flying a modified Great Circle arcing course from New York to London. As counterintuitive as it might look on a flat paper map, a curved route was shorter in distance than a straight line when flying across the blue sphere humans call home.

Because the two-engine plane didn't have enough flight time under its belt yet, it couldn't fly the ETOPS routes. It would have to stay within sixty miles of an airport as a safety precaution. In the irreverent world of aviation, the acronym ETOPS had morphed from its original meaning to Engines Turn or Passengers Swim. The FAA and ICAO were not amused by the change. Tonight, the flight would pass over the southern tip of Greenland. Next, they'd pass near Iceland, the island cleverly misnamed by the Vikings. Finally, just as the sun was peeking above the horizon, they would fly diagonally down over the United Kingdom into London.

Noelle made a PA. "As we continue our dinner service I'll be dimming the lights so those of you who wish to sleep can do so." The picture on the large screen had a momentary flicker. She dimmed the cabin lights and turned off the screen.

CHAPTER 9

MARK ARCHED HIS back and stretched both arms above his head to the sound of stiff joints cracking. He was trying to get the blood flowing again after sitting too long. Long overseas flights, combined with getting older, were taking a toll on Mark's body. Too proud to admit he was slowing down, Mark attributed his stiff muscles and poor-quality sleep to the job, and constantly bouncing back and forth between time zones. It certainly wasn't because he would now qualify for the senior citizen discount in a week. No, sir. *The damned FAA had no business telling me I would no longer be safe to fly passengers. I passed my last physical with flying colors. Every monthly piss test for alcohol had come back negative. Imagine the uproar* *if the government told doctors they couldn't practice after age sixty-five. They'd throw a fit! Pilots have many more lives in their hands at one time than any doctor ever could. Damn the FAA!*

Hoping his copilots didn't notice his stiffness, Mark asked, "Who wants to take the first break?"

They noticed.

"You go first, Mark. I'm good," Walter said.

"We'll keep an eye on things," Mo said.

"No, I'm fine."

"This will be your last landing in London, *ever.* You want to be well rested for it, don't you?" Mo added.

"We sure as hell do," Walter joked.

Mark could have used the break but waffled. "You guys sure? I should stay up here for the ocean crossing."

"Go ahead. We'll be just fine," Mo assured Mark.

"What the hell; it's been a long day. Buzz me in the crew bunk in two hours."

"Will do, boss," Mo responded.

Mark groaned slightly as he lifted himself up out of his seat. Mo slipped in to relieve him. Before walking out, Mark reminded them, "Call me if there are any problems."

Both copilots silently waved OK to Mark, having already shifted their attention to their iPads.

✈

MARK LOOKED THROUGH the peephole in the cockpit door to scan the area for any passengers before opening the door. The short, narrow hallway leading to the cockpit was clear. When he exited the cockpit, Mark stopped to steal a glance at Noelle. She was busy serving passengers dinner from a rolling metal cart. No stale mini pretzels in a bag for this crowd. The menu tonight had been orchestrated by a moody and abrasive celebrity chef. After polishing off the flamboyantly described courses of soup and salad, the main entrée had arrived. Reminiscent of the golden age of air travel, the pampered passengers had their choice of steak au poivre or lobster Thermidor. The few passengers who'd never ridden in first class before showed their excitement by ordering both. The meal was served on Lenox china expertly matched with a five-piece set of Christofle sterling silverware, all set on tray tables covered with fine white linen.

Mark watched Noelle unnoticed and smiled. His mind drifted back to when they first met. She was a newly hired flight attendant on her first day in training. Late to orientation class and lost in the maze-like training complex, Noelle had grabbed Mark as he walked by, asking for his help. She flashed a seductive smile that had worked on so many men and convinced him to take her to the right room. How could he say no to that smile and those crystal-blue eyes? Mark never believed in love at first sight—until that day.

The early years were great. It had been a love story worthy of a steamy romance novel: the indescribable high that comes from being head-over-heels in love, being affectionately nicknamed her Prince Charming, then the bond like no other that developed as their love matured.

After Mary came along, they were a real family. Now it all seemed like a distant memory. *How did I screw things up so badly? Noelle tried to get me to change my ways for years, but I wouldn't listen. Was I really that bad of a father and husband?* In a rare moment of introspection for such a stubborn, proud male, Mark silently answered his own question. As the mangled saying goes, "Time wounds all heels."

Noelle asked the passenger, "Would you like a roll with dinner, sir?"

He looked up. "Do you have wheat?"

When Noelle looked back at her cart she saw Mark watching her. Their eyes locked. They gazed tenderly at each other. Noelle smiled.

Suddenly, Tina popped up in front of Mark like an annoying fly that wouldn't go away. "Well, hello, Captain Mark."

With his view blocked and the smell of cheap perfume hard to ignore, Mark had no choice but to respond. "Hello, Ms. Reynolds."

"Why so formal? Please, call me Tina. Sooo...taking your break?

Mark just nodded as he tried to look past the nest of platinum hair blocking his view of Noelle.

"All by yourself? That doesn't sound like much fun. Any plans for our layover, Mark?"

"Why do you ask?"

"I've never seen London at night. I hear it's *very* romantic."

Looking down at Tina's shapely body, Mark slipped back into old habits. "Yes, Tina, now that you mention it, London is very romantic at night."

Tina arched a seductive eyebrow and lightly ran her hand down the length of Mark's arm. "Maybe you could give me a guided tour of the most stimulating parts, Captain?"

He could feel himself succumbing to the temptation presenting itself right in front of him. Before answering the not very thinly veiled question, Mark looked past Tina at Noelle.

She was glaring directly at him with fire in her eyes.

Noelle angrily plopped a roll down onto the passenger's plate and stormed away. "Men! You're all the same!"

"Whatever you have is fine," the confused passenger said apologetically.

With the subtlety of a sledgehammer, Tina poured on the flirting. "What do you say, Mark, interested? I'll make it worth your while."

Mark looked back at the empty spot Noelle had just been standing in, then at Tina. His desires battled with the regret he felt from hurting those closest to him. He could feel his willpower slowly melting away. Then Mark glanced down at the ring finger on his left hand. It was bare. The pale circle where his gold wedding band used to reside no longer existed.

The pain of regret won the internal battle.

He straightened up, looked Tina in the eyes, and said, "As tempting as your offer is, Ms. Reynolds, I'm afraid I'm going to pass."

Like flipping a switch, Tina's supposed interest in Mark vanished. Her temper quickly flared up. "Well screw it then, your loss." She stomped off.

Mark looked down again at his left hand. "Tell me about it."

MARK ENTERED THE pilot crew rest room. The tiny room was tucked along the left side of the plane, outside of the cockpit. It had one window and a narrow bed. Pilots used it to take turns resting on long flights. The short rest breaks didn't replace a good night's sleep, but they did help lessen the catastrophic effects fatigue can have on judgment and motor skills during demanding times—like landing at the busiest airport in Europe in the dense, early morning London fog. Passengers did appreciate their pilots being wide awake for the landing.

Mark turned on the light, plopped down on the edge of the bed, and removed his tie and shoes. Leaning forward with his elbows planted on his knees, he rested his chin on his folded hands, contemplating his uncertain future. "Thirty-five years. Now what?" With forced retirement from the airlines looming, Mark dreaded the thought of joining the ranks of everyday "ground pounders." He'd spent most of his adult life "slipping the surly bonds of earth" as the favorite poem of aviators, *High Flight*, so eloquently put it. Mark couldn't stomach the idea of seeing the same old scenery day after day. Even laying over in Milwaukee would be better than sitting at home with no real purpose in life. What bothered him most was the thought of spending the rest of his life alone.

He lay down on the bed and stared at the ceiling, hoping perhaps to find answers to his question. With no help coming from the ceiling panels, Mark rolled over and turned off the light. The stars in the heavens became clearly visible in the window, winking at him as if they knew something he didn't.

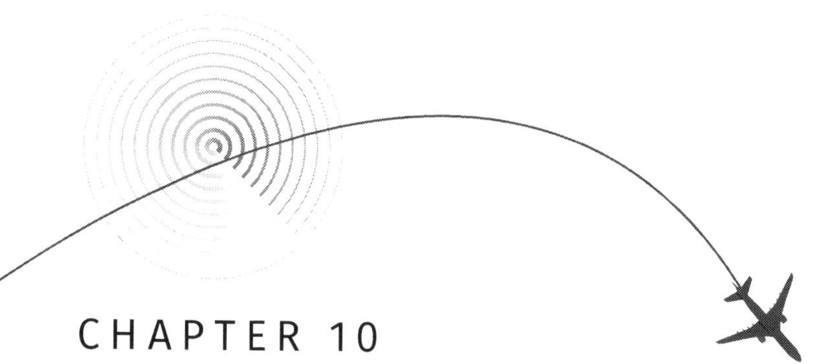

CHAPTER 10

IN THE CABIN, the gourmet dinner was over. Noelle had turned the temperature up a few degrees, increasing the likelihood the well-fed passengers would fall asleep and not bother the flight attendants. Drowsy passengers began converting their first-class seats into flat beds and drifting off to sleep under their six hundred-thread count, down-filled Schweitzer duvets. The Silicon Valley techies were wide awake, huddled around a laptop. They took full advantage of the free, top-shelf alcohol. The barely drinking-age geeks became more obnoxious and rowdy with every round. One flagged down a nearby flight attendant. "Stewardess, oh, stewardess."

She rolled her eyes at the use of that universally despised job title among flight attendants, then reluctantly came over. "Yes, sir, can I help you?"

"More Cristal for my associates and me. Also, I have a very important question." He leaned closer to her. "Where do I sign up for the mile-high club?" His buddies burst out laughing, high-fiving each other over the juvenile joke.

Not the least bit amused, she snapped, "Real original. Never heard *that one* before," and walked off.

A plain-looking young woman emerged from the bathroom, unaware she was the next target of the misogynistic geeks. One of them elbowed his buddy. "Dude, check out the hippie chick."

She looked the part: mousy, unkempt hair, tie-dye T-shirt, ragged bell bottom jeans with a peace sign sewn on, and the requisite Birkenstock sandals. Her questionable hygiene practices reinforced the stereotype.

As the woman walked by, a techie taunted her. "Nice bell bottoms."

She stopped and glared at him.

Piling on, another geek said, "Hey, flower child, you know you're on the wrong flight, don't you? We're going to London, not San Francisco."

Not the least bit intimidated, the woman got right up in his face. "Does your mommy know you snuck out of the basement tonight? Aren't you worried you'll get grounded?"

His face turned bright red from embarrassment. *How did she know I live with my mom?*

His buddy egged the techie on. "Bro, you gonna take that from a *chick*?"

The embarrassed geek struggled to put together a comeback. "Yeah, well, the 1960s called. It wants its clothes back."

Triumphant in this verbal battle, the "hippie chick" walked away, loudly saying, "Posers!"

Passengers nearby couldn't help but chuckle at the exchange.

Put in their place by a "chick," the techies grumbled to each other as they shrank back down into their seats and went back to their laptops.

A few rows back, Jan Frey looked around and admired the plush cabin. She nodded approvingly. "So, this is what I paid for."

Sitting next to Jan was Larry Morris, a kindly looking senior citizen. "Pardon?"

"My bank financed this plane. I chaired the loan committee."

"You're a banker?"

"Vice president of our New York office."

"Impressive."

"Biggest loan package in our history."

In the inexplicable world of aircraft financing, even financially struggling airlines can get approved for a fleet of shiny new airplanes—at a usurious interest rate, of course.

"That was a risky call on your part given Alpha's financial struggles lately."

"Maybe, but I'm confident the planes will help Alpha Airlines compete head to head with American and Delta for the high-yield international passengers out of New York. How about you? What do you do?"

"I was chief engineer for Tech Aerospace for thirty years."

"Was? Are you retired?"

Larry's pleasant expression evaporated. "That's what my back-stabbing boss called it. He tossed me out like yesterday's trash—for a man half my age. After *all* I did for them."

Jan's motherly instincts kicked in. "I'm so sorry to hear that. The corporate world can be pretty heartless sometimes."

"It's not right. A man needs to feel like his life's work was worth all the sacrifices. That it meant something." Larry shrugged. "I did talk Tech Aero into letting me go on this flight, so I'll give them that. I just had to see the end result of all those years of hard work. Even if nobody appreciated it."

"You worked on the Tech-Liner?"

Larry pointed to the techies. "Before those know-it-all punks took over the place like they own it, my team did all the design drawings for your plane."

"My plane..." Jan smiled as she thought about the words for a moment, then smugly said, "I like the sound of that." Then she added wistfully, "Just wish I didn't spend so much of my life on them."

Larry caught her drift. "How many kids do you have?"

"Two. A boy, eight years old, and a girl, six. Would you like to see pictures of them?"

Wishing he hadn't asked, but too late to take back his words, he forced a grin and said, "Sure."

Jan fished her smartphone out of her purse. She swiped through vacation pictures until she got to one with only her children in it. She pointed the screen toward Larry. "This is my son, Erik. All boy. Never stops moving. My daughter's name is—"

Noelle walked up and glanced over Jan's shoulder. "Cute kids. Your family?"

"Yes, they are," Jan said proudly. "This kind man was nice enough to pretend he wanted to see my pictures."

"Not at all. You have a beautiful family," Larry quickly blurted out.

Charlotte walked up, ignoring the picture. "When you get a minute, Noelle, I need your help in the back galley. Damned ovens are acting up."

"Okay, in a sec," she told Charlotte. "Are you traveling alone?" Noelle asked Larry.

"Yes. I'm a widower." His eyes moistened as he continued. "I lost my Millie to cancer three years ago." It was obvious the cruel disease that had taken his beloved wife had also left an aching hole in his heart.

Noelle reached out and gently patted Larry's arm. "I'm so sorry. I know how it feels. I lost my mother to breast cancer when I was in high school. Cancer misérable!"

Larry nodded. "Miserable indeed, ma chère. Miserable indeed. Before she got sick, Millie and I loved to travel the world together. Now, with her gone, I just mope around my gloomy old house all day. So, I figured I'd go on this one last trip."

"Good for you," Jan said.

"Who knows, a handsome guy like yourself, maybe you'll find a new lady friend," Noelle added.

"Nobody's going to want to hang around with an old coot like me. To be honest, I wasn't always the best husband."

"Play the field then. Besides, marriage is overrated if you ask me," Noelle said.

Larry looked up at Noelle. He saw the unmistakable signs of a broken heart in her crystal-blue eyes—notwithstanding the bravado in her statement. "Young lady, as I look back now with 20/20 hindsight, despite all the ups and downs, I'd give anything to have my Millie back. It's rare to find your one true soul mate in this life. I was fortunate to find mine. Life just isn't the same without her." He added a very strategically thought out bit of humility. "Then again, I'm just an old fool. What do I know. You're probably right."

Noelle pondered his hard-earned wisdom for a moment. Then she asked, "Can I get you anything while I'm here?"

Jan shook her head. "No, I'm fine."

"Thank you, no," Larry answered.

With a faraway look in her eyes, Noelle said, "If you'll excuse me, I need to go fix something."

CHAPTER 11

MARK'S SLUMBER BECAME more and more fitful as he tossed and turned in the crew bunk. Suddenly, he threw back the covers and bolted upright with his eyes closed and heart racing. He pleaded, "Dad, no! I don't want to go in the water!"

A strange buzzing noise interrupted Mark's pleading.

Floating in the dark above Mark's head, a red button flashed. Mark shook his head, rubbed his eyes, and looked up. He snapped back to present day, safe and sound in the bed. Mark pushed the button, stopping the buzzing sound. The red light, labeled COCKPIT, stayed lit, providing the only light in the room. He rubbed more sleep from his eyes then stared drowsily out the window at the beauty of the cosmos. The stars in the heavens sparkled like diamonds randomly tossed on a carpet of black velvet.

Mark gazed at the stars, contemplating the vastness of the universe and his soon-to-be new place in it. After a few moments, he abruptly narrowed his gaze. Mark cocked his head to the side with a confused look on his face. He looked out the left, then the right side of the window desperately searching for something. *Where is it?* He rubbed his eyes again. *Am I awake or still dreaming?* Positive he was fully awake, a look of panic washed over his face. The lingering feeling of drowsiness was replaced by a rush of adrenalin. Mark put on his tie, stabbed his feet into his loafers, then bolted out of the room toward the cockpit.

CHAPTER 12

MARK BURST INTO the fully lit cockpit, ruining his night vision. He squinted and raised his right hand in front of his eyes to temporarily block the light.

Mo had his feet propped up, reading yesterday's *USA Today*. When he saw Mark, he stashed it away. "That was quick."

"Where are we?" Mark asked with alarm in his voice.

Pointing to the arcing course line displayed on the screen, Mo said, "Approaching Shannon's airspace. Why?"

"I asked you guys to wake me up in two hours, not four."

Walter looked over at Mo. With no help coming, he looked back at Mark to explain. “It was pretty quiet up here, so we figured we’d let you sleep a little longer.”

“Something’s not right. Recheck our position.”

Walter and Mo tapped on their screens, requesting an update on their position. The powerful navigation computer instantly recalculated the plane’s location. Identical navigation information displayed on each screen.

“Right on course,” Mo said.

“Same here.” Walter asked nervously, “What’s up, Mark?”

“Send Gander a CPDLC message asking them to verify our position in their system.”

“If you say so.” Walter didn’t bother to hide his annoyance. He reluctantly typed the message on the keypad. A response from Gander Oceanic ATC popped up on the screen after a few seconds. ON COURSE, ON ALTITUDE. Walter showed Mark the message. “Like we said.”

Mark shook his head. “No...something’s not...something’s not right.” He motioned to Mo. “Switch out.”

Mo climbed out of the captain’s seat. Mark sat down and strapped in.

“What’s going on, Mark?” Walter asked.

“The stars...they’re not...”

“The stars are not what?” Mo asked.

Mark directed Walter. “Turn down the lights, I want to look at the stars.”

Walter's and Mo's faces changed from annoyance to concern. Walter turned the cockpit lights down very low. The universe filled the view out the windows. Without any man-made light or pollution obstructing the view, billions of stars were clearly visible.

Mark pointed out the window on his left side. "It should be right there."

"What should be?" both copilots ask in unison.

"Polaris. It should be right over there."

Standing behind Mark's seat, Mo craned his neck to look out the window. "Maybe it moved."

"It never moves. The North Star is always on the left side of the plane when flying east." Mark asked suspiciously, "What the hell did you guys do up here while I was gone? Why did you take so long to wake me?"

"Hold on there. What are you implying?" Mo shot back.

"I can't see the North Star out any of our windows. That means it's behind us, and we are headed south, not east."

Mo had enough. "All right, this is bullshit."

"Damn right this is bull," Walter agreed.

Mo continued. "The instruments show we're on course. Gander verified we're on course—"

Mark interrupted. "In the flight planning room... you guys shook hands...I'm gone for four hours... now we're..."

"*That's* what you're talking about?" Mo questioned.

Walter explained. "My wife is pregnant with number four. We need a bigger car. I bought Mo's old one."

Mark's head cocked suspiciously to one side, not sure if he was being conned. He scanned the faces of the two pilots, the only people in the cockpit for the last four hours, for any telltale signs of dishonesty.

Mo clarified. "I sold Walter my car. We shook on it. What the hell did you think we were agreeing to?"

Walter couldn't believe what they were being accused of. "Jesus, Mark. You think we would..."

"You think we would do...*that*! Based on a damned star!" Mo added.

Mark tried to make amends. "Guys, I owe you a huge apology. I had no idea that's what you were—"

Walter cut him off. "So you accuse us of sending our plane out into the middle of nowhere?"

"I screwed up big time. I never should have accused you guys of that. But I'm *telling you*, something's not right. I've done this run hundreds of times. We need to verify our location."

"*Mark*, we already did. We're on course," Mo fumed.

Walter tried to reason with Mark. "The GPS shows we're on course. Gander said we're on course. What more do you want?"

"Both the GPS and SatComm radio use the same antenna. What if it's damaged?"

"Now you're grasping at straws, Mark. Based on *celestial navigation* for God's sake," Mo countered.

"That's it!" Mark slid the work table out in front of himself and unfolded his map. "I haven't practiced this since I was in the Air Force."

Mo saw where this was going. "You've *got* to be kidding me."

Mark took smug pleasure in knowing a navigation method used since ancient times when Babylonian astronomers first applied the discipline of mathematics to their observations could prove the world's most advanced navigation computers wrong. "The stars never fail. Not like friggin' technology." Mark searched the night sky then pointed out the center window. "Okay, there's Orion."

He drew a line on the map.

"That's Cancer over there. No wait, that's Virgo...I think." He drew another line on the map.

"Hey, Magellan."

Mark turned to see Mo holding up his smartphone. "Try using this. It's the Sky Tracker app. You've heard of apps, haven't you? All the constellations are on it."

"Really?" Mark replied sheepishly.

"Really." Mo looked at Walter and rolled his eyes.

Embarrassed, but grateful for the assistance, Mark said, "Point it that way. What does it say?"

Mo carefully examined the app then pointed toward the night sky. "Okay, that's Gemini over there."

Mark drew another line on the map. "I need at least two more to get an accurate position." He searched for more recognizable constellations. Suddenly the plane flew into a thick cloud layer. "Dammit!" Mark fumed.

In the dark, they never saw the clouds coming. In an instant, their view was reduced from millions of light-years to a few feet.

"Let's climb. Maybe we can get above the clouds," Walter suggested.

Mark immediately vetoed the idea. "No! Hold on. We're not even sure where we are. We might climb into another plane. We're better off staying at our last known altitude—for now."

"Good point." Walter saw the wisdom in that decision.

"Can you tell our location yet, Mark?" Mo asked.

Mark connected the lines then drew a probable location circle on the map. He showed it to the copilots.

The circle covered the entire Atlantic Ocean.

Mo shook his head. "So much for that."

Mark told Walter, "Drop down the standby compass. It's the only thing on this stupid plane that's not connected to a computer."

The old-style compass—the type used for centuries for rudimentary navigation, but extraneous on a modern jet—was tucked up out of the way in the ceiling panel above the two front windows, out of view of the pilots. Walter reached up and pulled the compass down into view.

Everyone's jaws dropped.

The vertical line on the glass window was directly over a bold letter *S*.

"We're headed straight south," Walter gasped.

Mo refused to believe his own eyes. "I don't care what that damned thing says. Three of the most sophisticated navigation computers on the planet say we're on course. ATC said we're on course. It must be broken."

"The stars don't lie, Mo."

"He's right, Mo. We're off course," Walter agreed.

"I'm turning east." Mark rotated the autopilot heading selector knob to 090 degrees and pushed it in to enter the new heading. The plane didn't turn. He pushed the knob in again. Nothing happened.

"Push it harder," Walter suggested.

Mark pushed it again. The autopilot did not respond. "Screw this, I'll turn it myself." Mark reached up to the glare shield and turned off the autopilot master switch so he could hand-fly the plane. The autopilot stayed engaged. "What the hell..." Mark flipped the switch again and again. "The autopilot disconnect isn't working." Mark tried moving his control stick. It wouldn't budge. He pulled harder. It was solid as a rock.

Mark asked Walter to try moving his control stick. His was frozen as well.

Mark reached over and pulled the two throttles back to idle. The engines continued to hum along unchanged.

He yelled at his copilots. "What the hell did you guys do?!"

"Nothing, I swear!" Walter replied, panicking.

Mark instructed Walter, "Declare a Mayday! Send a message to ATC. Tell them we've lost all control over our aircraft."

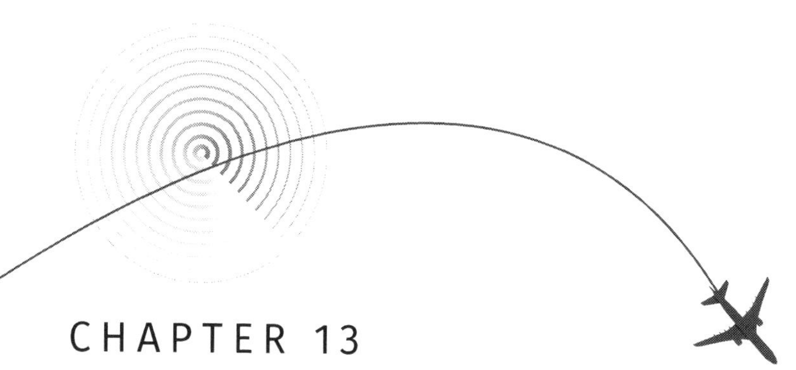

CHAPTER 13

THE ALPHA AIRLINES dispatch office was in a state of chaos. Anxious dispatchers furiously typed away at their computers and made frantic phone calls to department supervisors listed on the CRC (Crisis Response Checklist).

Peter Mills, chief operating officer for Alpha Airlines, had been awakened with the bad news thirty minutes ago. He ran into the dispatch office haphazardly dressed in jeans and a wrinkled Princeton sweatshirt. Bill, the dispatcher assigned to the Tech-Liner flight, saw the disheveled man and waved. "Mr. Mills, over here."

"I got here as soon as I could. Bring me up to speed."

Bill recapped. “Gander Oceanic lost contact with them shortly after they left Canadian airspace.”

“Did they send out any type of distress signal?”

“Nothing. Nobody has been able to reach them on 121.5, the emergency Guard channel. No 7500 transponder squawk indicating a hijacking. No indication of any trouble at all. It’s like they vanished into thin air,” Bill said.

“Damn, not another Malaysian airlines. Not with our plane,” Mills told Bill. “Wake up the chairman of the board. And where is Mr. Andrews? Why isn’t he here?”

Bill shook his head. “Don’t bother. They’re both on the plane.”

HAMPTON AND ANDREWS were enjoying free drinks in the onboard lounge. Andrews raised his glass and said, “I’m glad you could join us for the inaugural flight, Mr. Chairman. Here’s to Alpha Airlines and what I predict will be a very bright future.”

When Hampton only halfheartedly clinked his glass against Andrews’s, the CEO realized he had overestimated the amount of confidence the chairman had for his leadership. He quickly grabbed the bottle from the bar and poured another three fingers into the Hampton’s glass. “I realize the board has its misgivings about the size of the Tech-Liner order.”

Hampton warned Andrews. "On behalf of the board, I need to remind you there's a lot riding on this trip. You are gambling the future of the airline on this damned plane."

"I guarantee you will be very happy with my decision," Andrews boasted.

Hampton knocked back the last remnants of his Jameson Irish whiskey, then scowled, "For your sake, and the sake of your generous compensation plan, I better be."

"It's money well spent, I assure you." Then, with a completely straight face, he said, "Thirty-five million dollars a year is a bargain compared to the value I bring to the table." Hampton's dubious-sounding grunt was his only reply.

The flight attendants, unaware of their predicament, casually walked around checking on passengers.

The small, sour-faced Dr. Wong skimmed through today's edition of the *People's Daily* newspaper on his laptop while he scribbled notes on a yellow legal pad.

The Silicon Valley techies continued soaking up the free booze, huddled around a laptop playing video games.

The Russian was still a jerk.

MARK FURROWED HIS brow and took a sip of his coffee. There was an almost imperceptible shaking in his hand. Drawing on his decades of experience as a pilot and hours of incredibly realistic training in Level D simulators, Mark methodically took stock of their grim situation. “All right, let’s work the problem. Fuel—how much do we have?”

Walter checked his screen. “A little more than one hour.”

“Shit. Okay, I need one of you guys to go down into the electronics compartment and see if you can find anything abnormal down there. Anything that might explain what the hell is going on.”

Walter started to volunteer, but Mo overrode him with a hand to his shoulder. “No, Walter, I’ll do it.” Mo unlocked the floor hatch, pulled it open, and descended the ladder.

THE HOT ELECTRONICS compartment was dimly lit by one small light mounted on the wall. The glow from the computers was the only other source of light. A faint hum could be heard coming from the racks of electronic equipment. Standing on the narrow walkway, Mo pulled a pen-size flashlight out of his shirt pocket and shone the thin beam around. He muttered, “What the hell am I supposed to be looking for? I’ve never been down here.” His flashlight beam swept by each of the racks, looking for something unusual. He shook his head in resignation. “I don’t see shit.”

“You see anything, Mo?” Mark yelled from the cockpit.

Mo turned and yelled back toward the hatch, "I don't see shit!" Mo gave up on the pointless search and shuffled back along the walkway to the hatch. Before starting up the ladder he decided to take one last look back. Something caught his eye.

Mo narrowed his gaze trying to focus. He pointed his flashlight toward the far end of the compartment. "What the hell?" He yelled toward the hatch, "Hold on, I think I see something." Mo squeezed back through the racks, intently staring at one of the computers. He was so focused on the alarming discovery that he didn't notice when his belt buckle caught on a cable. Feeling resistance, and assuming he was caught on a rack, Mo yanked himself forward while trying to keep his eyes locked on the computer.

The cable ripped loose.

A pyrotechnic shower of sparks engulfed Mo. He stumbled backward and collapsed onto the walkway. His flashlight landed beside his head, illuminating the dreadful look of shock, eternally fixed on his dead face.

THE BACK GALLEY and the aft end of the passenger cabin suddenly went dark.

A startled woman let out a piercing scream.

LIGHTS IN THE cockpit flickered. Walter jumped out of his seat and stuck his head down into the access hatch. "Mo! Mohammed!"

The one wall light in the electronics compartment had blown out. Walter couldn't see more than few feet due to the dense smoke that filled the compartment.

CHARLOTTE RAN UP to Noelle. "Honey, what happened?"

"I don't know." She picked up the handset at the flight attendant panel and punched the cockpit button.

MARK PICKED UP.

"We just lost power to the aft part of the cabin, Mark. What's going on?" Noelle said.

He could hear the concern in Noelle's voice loud and clear. "Get Andrews and come up here—now! And block access to the cockpit door with two galley carts."

"Why Mark? Tell me what happened."

"Just do it!"

THE ALARMING INSTRUCTIONS momentarily paralyzed Noelle. Then her years of training kicked in. She directed Charlotte, “Find Mike Andrews, and get him up here. Tell him it’s an emergency. And don’t let anyone near the cockpit door!”

CHAPTER 14

WALTER'S HEAD HUNG down in the access hatch. Thick, toxic smoke stung his eyes. Rubbing them only made it worse. The smoke prevented him from keeping his head down for more than a few seconds. Each time he came up, he violently coughed, trying to clear his lungs. He tried to clear the thick smoke by waving his hands back and forth across the opening. When that didn't work, Walter grabbed a printed checklist and waved it across the hatch.

"What's happening? Can you see Mo?"

Walter held his breath and looked down into the compartment again. He could barely make out the shape of a man on the walkway. Walter lifted his head out of the hatch and coughed out the answer. "Mo's lying on the walkway." Walter shook his head. "He's not moving."

A loud DING shattered the tension. Mark pulled up the feed from the cockpit entrance camera on the center screen. A fisheye view from the ceiling mounted camera outside the cockpit door showed Noelle and Andrews anxiously waiting. Two galley carts behind them barricaded the only path into the cockpit.

Mark pressed a button on the aft end of the center console. Electric deadbolts released, and the cockpit door popped open. Noelle and Andrews looked around for any suspicious passengers that might be lurking nearby, then hurried through the grenade-proof door, securely closing it behind them.

Andrews looked down at Walter, on his knees next to the hatch. "What the hell is going on, Smith? The lights went out and—"

Mark cut him off. "Shut the hell up. I don't have time for your crap. We've got a serious problem. I have no control over my plane. Everything's frozen. We're off course, extremely low on fuel thanks to you, and one of my copilots is downstairs in the electronics compartment. I think he's been electrocuted."

Noelle's eyes widened as she clasped her hand over her mouth. "Oh my God!"

Andrews failed to grasp the danger they were in. "Dammit, Smith, I knew I shouldn't have trusted you with this flight."

Enraged at the unfair indictment of her ex, Noelle turned around and slapped Andrews across the face. "Look here, you son of a bitch, Mark is the best damned pilot this airline has. If there's a problem, you're lucky he's in the left seat."

Andrews was temporarily stunned by the brazen act. Then he appeared ready to strike back.

Mark ignored the ego-boosting endorsement from his ex and jumped into the fray. "Okay, everyone calm down. Take a breath. Mike, go down into the electronics compartment with Walter, and bring Mo up to the cockpit. Noelle, get all the flight attendants together in the front galley, out of sight of the passengers. Quietly tell them what's going on. But *do not* tell the passengers anything."

CHAPTER 15

NOELLE QUICKLY WALKED down the aisle ushering the flight attendants toward the front galley. She did an Oscar-worthy acting job not letting the fear she was feeling show on her face.

As Noelle neared Basara he put his arm across the aisle, blocking her path. "I demand to know what is going on. Why am I sitting in the dark?"

Noelle fell back on her years of experience dealing with demanding passengers. "There's no cause for alarm, sir. It appears one of the circuit breakers popped a fuse, causing the current to flow backward and flood the empennage. That triggered the lights to temporarily go out."

Basara nodded suspiciously. “I see.” Not surprisingly, Prince Omar bin Basara was not well versed in matters such as electrical wiring (or anything else requiring manual labor). Noelle could have told him the Flux Capacitor was acting up, and he would have bought it.

“When will my lights be turned back on?” he whined.

“It shouldn’t be too much longer, sir.” Noelle took Basara’s arm and firmly placed it back on his armrest, then continued down the aisle.

THE TWO MEN approached Mo as he lay motionless on the walkway. Walter bent down and gently shook him. “Mo? Mo? Are you all right?”

Andrews stepped over Mo and placed two fingers on the man’s carotid artery. He bluntly declared, “He’s dead.”

Walter’s head sank.

Andrews waved Walter over. “Help me pick him up.” He wrapped his arms under Mo’s back while Walter grabbed Mo’s bent legs. They struggled to lift the heavy, lifeless body. Bent over, the two men did a duck-like shuffle, carrying the dead body down the narrow walkway.

Walter’s sweaty grip on Mo’s legs slipped. As he flailed trying to stop Mo from falling from his grasp, his glasses were knocked off his face. “My glasses!”

Andrews dropped Mo with a thud. “Forget your damned glasses. Let’s drag him the rest of the way.”

They each grabbed an arm and unceremoniously dragged the corpse the last few yards. Together they lifted Mo's body up to the hatch.

MARK WAS WAITING. He grabbed Mo under the arms and helped lift the dead body up out of the electronics compartment. As he lifted, Mark looked directly into Mo's open, terror-filled eyes—a ghastly image that would be seared in his mind forever.

None of the men said a word as they placed Mo in a jumpseat, strapping him in tightly. Mark took his captain's jacket out of the coat closet and solemnly draped it over the dead man, covering his ghostly expression.

Andrews went on the attack again, pointing his finger in Mark's face. "Smith, I want to know what the hell is *really* going on. Why didn't you call me sooner?"

Mark was stunned at his insensitivity. "Really going on? I have a *dead copilot*, that's what's *really* going on!"

Walter stepped in, trying to play peacemaker. "Ease up, man, he's only been up here a few minutes."

"A few minutes? Where the hell were you?"

Mark tried to explain. "Look, against my better judgement, I took the first break. My copilots were trying to be nice and let me sleep an extra few hours—"

"Everything's going to hell, and you're *sleeping*?"

Walter defended his captain. "It was our fault, not his."

Andrews headed for the cockpit door. "I've got to inform the chairman of the board."

"Be sure to tell him what a savvy businessman you are," Mark said dryly.

Andrews stiffened inside his three-thousand-dollar suit. He turned back and glared at Mark. "Smith, get me and this plane on dry land." He dashed out of the cockpit.

Walter looked back at the door. "What an ass."

"Couldn't fly worth a damn, either," Mark added.

"I don't think he'll be giving you any more crap soon. At least not within arm's reach of Noelle, that is." Walter chuckled, waited a few seconds, then probed, "I gotta ask, Mark. You and she have something going on?"

"She's my ex."

"Remind me not to piss her off."

"Trust me, you don't want to."

CHAPTER 16

MIKE ANDREWS CAME out of the cockpit with a terrified look on his ashen face. Hampton grabbed Andrews by the arm and demanded, "What the hell is going on? The passengers are asking questions, and the flight attendants won't tell me a damned thing."

Looking around, Andrews saw a planeload of curious passengers staring directly at him. He forced a weak smile back at them then leaned toward Hampton and whispered, "I need to talk to you in private." He gestured toward the back of the cabin.

As they started down the aisle, Jan Frey stopped them and calmly asked, "Is there a problem, gentlemen?" Her eyes betrayed her real feelings of worry.

Andrews brushed her off with a quick lie. "Everything's fine, ma'am. Just a little glitch."

Reaching the darkened aft end of the cabin, Hampton snarled, "Glitch, my ass! What the hell is wrong with *your* plane Andrews? I want to know everything."

Andrews looked left and right. In a hushed voice he said, "I think we've got a rogue captain on our hands."

"*What*?!"

Just as Andrews tried to justify his wild accusation, a passenger came out of the nearby lavatory, interrupting their conversation. It was Laurent's executive assistant. She looked warily at the men as she tucked the last piece of her blouse into her skirt.

Andrews immediately clammed up and gave her a dismissive nod.

She nodded politely back. Suspicious as to why the two Alpha Airline bigwigs were huddled together whispering in the dark, she slowly sauntered up the aisle, hoping to overhear their conversation. She stopped at Dr. Wong's seat and struck up a conversation. After listening for a moment, Wong turned back and glared at Andrews and Hampton, unwittingly ruining her ruse. Seeing they were onto her attempt to eavesdrop, she moved on.

Andrews waited for her to get well out of earshot. When satisfied she was, he continued. "I just talked to Captain Smith. He gave me this cock-and-bull story about the plane being wildly off course. He said we're short on gas, the controls are frozen, and he has no control over the plane. But I'm not buying it. And get this, one of his copilots is *dead*. Smith *claims* he was accidentally electrocuted."

"Dead! How do you know Smith is not telling the truth? Maybe there *is* something wrong with the plane. And how the hell can we be short on gas?"

"This plane is the—"

François Laurent unexpectedly came out of the same lavatory as his assistant—with a big grin on his face. When he turned to walk away he ended up sandwiched between Andrews and Hampton. Surprised to see them, he fumbled a guilt-laced greeting. "Alexander. Andrews. How nice to see you."

Hampton rolled his eyes. "François."

Andrews looked at François, up the aisle, then back at François. "Do you mind?"

"Certainly." Embarrassed, Laurent scurried away.

Andrews continued. "This is the most high-tech airliner on the planet. It doesn't just get itself lost. I was a pilot, remember? I know how these things work. It's got to be Smith."

Hampton started up the aisle. "I need to talk to Captain Smith."

Andrews practically jumped in front of the chairman. "I don't think that's a good idea."

"Why the hell not?"

"Smith was acting very strange when I was in the cockpit. You might upset him more." Andrews avoided eye contact with Hampton as he said, "Oh no. Now it all makes sense."

"What?"

"Captain Smith told me back at JFK that he was going to make this a memorable last trip."

"Last trip?"

"I wish it wasn't so, but the FAA is forcing him to retire after this trip. He's furious about it."

Terror flashed across Hampton's face. "Oh my God! You're not suggesting...?"

Andrews said nothing to discourage the conclusion Hampton had drawn. Both men hurried off.

Out of the shadows, a passenger slowly emerged from the nearby galley.

He had overheard everything.

The passenger, a used car salesman with slicked back hair and a gold front tooth, clutched a handful of small liquor bottles pilfered from the unattended galley. He'd already downed the contents of six. He weaved his way back to his seat and plopped down. Reeking of alcohol, he confided in the stranger sitting next to him. "We're in grave danger."

Waving away the intoxicated breath of his seatmate, the annoyed man asked, "What are you talking about?"

Thinking he was whispering, the salesman leaned over and loudly said, "The captain is trying to kill us."

CHAPTER 17

WALTER LOOKED AT Mark. "I dropped my glasses down in the electronics compartment. You okay up here for a few minutes while I go get them?"

Mark nodded. "Go ahead. I'll be just fine."

Walter unlocked the hatch door and climbed down the ladder into the compartment.

Mark turned and watched Walter until he was out of sight.

WALTER FUMBLED AROUND in the dark, looking for his glasses. The live wire that had killed Mo blocked the walkway as it swayed back and forth like a deadly viper ready to attack. Careful not to touch the metal racks, he extended his leg and used the rubber sole on his shoe to tuck the wire harmlessly out of the way. A few yards ahead he spotted his badly cracked glasses. After putting them on, the dimly lit compartment came into focus. Something up ahead caught Walter's eye. He maneuvered over to a computer rack at the far end of the compartment. Walter clearly saw what had aroused Mo's suspicion before he died. "What the hell?"

MARK SLIPPED OUT of his seat and went over to the open hatch. He looked down the opening to see if Walter was nearby. Not seeing him, Mark knelt beside the hatch with his hand resting on the door.

Walter poked his head up through the hatch, breathless. "You're not going to believe this. There's a Brain plugged into the master computer."

"A Brain? Who the...? Go pull it out! Pull it out!"

WALTER HURRIED BACK along the narrow walkway to the master computer. The small electronic module—the Brain—was inserted into a recessed slot on the face of the computer. He lifted the clear plastic cover, pinched the end of the module with his thumb and pointer finger, and pulled. It wouldn't budge. He tried using both hands to get a better grip on the small module. The Brain would not come out.

Walter glanced down at the walkway through his cracked glasses. The reason the Brain refused to budge was right at his feet. An empty tube of Super Glue lay on the walkway.

He rushed back to the hatch with the empty tube. "Mark, the Brain has been glued into its socket. I'll never be able to get it out."

Mark's normally unflappable emotions took a hit. "Jesus Christ! Who the hell would do that?" The search for the culprit would have to wait. Mark methodically racked his low-tech brain for a solution to their predicament. He looked around then yanked the heavy-duty crash axe off the cockpit wall mount. "Here, break the damned thing off with this."

Walter waved the axe away. "Won't work. The Brain isn't sticking out far enough."

Mark desperately searched for another way to prevent certain death for his crew and passengers.

"Try this."

Mark handed Walter his cup of coffee.

Confused, he asked, "What am I supposed to do with this?"

"Pour it on the Brain. Maybe we can short it out."

With no better idea, Walter headed back into the electronics compartment carefully carrying the hot cup of coffee. When he reached the master computer, Walter poured some coffee on the Brain. Other than get his polished black leather shoes wet, nothing happened. He poured a little more. His shoes were now soaked with coffee but the indicator lights on the end of the Brain module continued to blink. "Screw this." Walter dumped the rest of the coffee onto the Brain. A loud pop was heard then a puff of white smoke rose from the module. The indicator lights on the end of the module went out. Astonished, Walter yelled, "It worked!"

WHEN MARK HEARD the shout from below he looked up at the three cockpit screens. The information on them instantly changed. Mark scrambled back into the left seat. He closely examined the new information presented before him. An entirely new reality appeared. Mark stared at the screens in disbelief. "Holy shit!"

They were in the middle of the Atlantic Ocean.

A satellite radio transmission suddenly blasted over the cockpit speaker.

"Alpha One, Gander Oceanic, how do you read? Alpha One, if you hear Oceanic, respond immediately!"

The blaring radio transmission slapped Mark back to reality. He grabbed the hand mic. "Oceanic, this is Alpha One. I read you loud and clear."

THE DIMLY LIT air traffic control room was filled with computer consoles, the green glow of radar screens, and desperate controllers. The Gander Oceanic controller almost jumped out of his seat. "I got 'em!" he yelled to his coworkers. The controller keyed his mic. "Alpha One, this is Oceanic. What the hell are you guys doing up there? You vanished into thin air over four hours ago!"

MARK TRIED TO project calm as he transmitted his response. "Oceanic, Alpha One declaring a Mayday. We've had a serious malfunction up here. Stand by for status."

Walter jumped back into the right seat and stared in disbelief at his screen. "Oh God. No."

CHAPTER 18

THE GREEN DATA block identifying Alpha One reappeared on the Gander Oceanic air traffic controller's screen. The visibly relieved controller said, "Alpha One, your aircraft is transmitting your position again. We see you on our screen. Stand by for..." The stunned controller dropped his cigarette into his lap. "Alpha One, you're over a thousand miles off course, headed straight south! Has the cockpit been compromised? Are you experiencing a hijacking?"

"NEGATIVE, THE COCKPIT has not been compromised. We have not been...I...stand by, Gander, we're still trying to sort things out up here." Mark directed Walter, "Punch in direct London."

He typed the airport code for London Heathrow airport, EGLL, into the navigation computer. A warning message immediately flashed red on their screens: INSUFFICIENT FUEL.

"Crap. Try Shannon, Ireland."

The same disheartening red message came up on the screen. Walter reported, "Not even close."

"Try Keflavik, Iceland."

Same flashing red message.

Walter stated the obvious, "We're screwed."

"There's got to be somewhere we can..." Mark racked his brain. "The Azores!"

"Where?"

"The Azores. It's a small chain of islands owned by Portugal in the middle of the Atlantic. I flew in there once when I was flying C-141s in the Air Force." Mark unfolded his map and circled the tiny Azores Islands. "There's a runway there. Punch in Lajes Field, Azores. The code is Lima Papa Lima Alpha."

Walter quickly typed it in.

The alarming message INSUFFICIENT FUEL again flashed red on their screens.

"Still short."

"How short?"

"Computer said we'll run out of fuel fifty miles before we reach the runway."

Mark thought for a second then made an irrevocable decision that sealed their fate. "Set a course direct to Lajes Field. We don't have any better options." Mark thumbed his mic button. "Oceanic, we're diverting to the Azores."

THE CONTROLLER CUPPED his hand over his microphone and yelled, "They're headed for the Azores!"

THE TECH-LINER HEADED south until it vanished into the vast night sky.

CHAPTER 19

MARK FINALLY UNDERSTOOD the true meaning of the old saying about life as an airline pilot: Hours and hours of boredom, punctuated by moments of sheer terror. *Yeah, no kidding. Time to earn my pay.*

Mark briefed Walter on the plan of action. "You're flying. Go to economy cruise power setting to save fuel. Review the emergency checklist for ditching. I'll coordinate everything else. Any questions?"

"Got it."

"Oceanic, this is Captain Smith. We are proceeding direct to Lajes Field. Notify the airport manager. Tell him we're going to need all the emergency equipment they've got."

"ROGER, ALPHA ONE." The controller turned to his supervisor and yelled, "Call Lajes! Tell them they have an emergency aircraft inbound! Get everything they have ready!"

WALTER TURNED TO Mark and asked, "What'll we tell the passengers?"

Mark shook his head. "Nothing. Not until we know what we're up against. Disable passenger flight progress screens. That will buy us some time before we have to break the bad news."

ON TERCEIRA ISLAND, a man in a spartan shack was sound asleep in his bed.

The phone on the nightstand rang.

He ignored it.

It continued to ring.

He grumbled at the annoying device then rolled over.

The ringing continued.

He picked up the receiver then angrily slammed it down.

Five seconds later the phone rang again.

He finally gave in and picked up. "Lajes airport manager. This better be important."

The man listened for a moment then bolted out of bed.

"GOING TO THE economy power setting helped. We're down to twenty-five miles short of the runway," Walter said optimistically.

Mark keyed his mic. "Oceanic, it looks like we are going to be twenty-five miles short of Lajes. Divert all ships in the vicinity to twenty-five miles north of the Azores.

THE CONTROLLER RESPONDED, "Way ahead of you, Alpha One. We have the coast guard on the line right now. They are contacting ships as we speak. They say the nearest ship should arrive in that area in approximately four hours."

Mark's response, including the sound of a fist hitting the cockpit glare shield, blared over the controller's speaker, "Four hours! We're looking at ditching in the Atlantic Ocean. At night. In *January*! Anyone who survives the ditching will never last four hours!"

The controller shrugged. "I'm sorry, Captain. I hear what you're saying. We're doing everything we can down here to help you."

MARK'S BROAD SHOULDERS sagged. "I know you are. Sorry. Things are a little tense up here. Patch me through to Alpha Airlines dispatch office. I'm sure they're wondering what's going on."

Over the cockpit speaker, Oceanic responded, "Will do. Stand by while we make the connection. Also, when you get a chance, please pass along the number of souls on board."

Mark detested it when air traffic controllers used that word—souls—to ask for the total number of passengers and crew on an airplane during an emergency. Souls had such a ghoulish connotation to it.

"We have 110...souls on board."

CHAPTER 20

THE DISPATCH OFFICE was a cacophony of ringing telephones, radio chatter, and heated discussions. Supervisors from every department gathered in the room, busy executing their respective accident response protocols.

A buzzer sounded at Bill's dispatcher console. "It's Gander Oceanic," he said apprehensively, looking back at the crowd.

The room immediately quieted down.

Bill picked up a red handset and took a deep breath, expecting the worst. "Go ahead, Gander."

He listened intently for a few moments. "You did?" Bill jumped up and yelled, "They found 'em!"

The room exploded with applause. High-fives were thrown all around.

Bill waved at everyone to quiet down. "Patch them through, Gander." Bill nervously tapped his fingers while he waited to be connected to the wayward aircraft.

Mills directed Bill. "Put them on speaker."

He flipped a switch on his console and hung up the handset. The only sound coming across the speaker was an irritating static. Bill queried into his headset microphone, "Alpha One, this is dispatch. How do you read?"

Nothing but static came from the speaker.

Bill swallowed hard. "Alpha One, are you there?"

Seconds—which seemed like minutes—ticked away without a response from the plane.

"Alpha One, this is dispatch. Do you copy?"

Mark's metallic sounding voice finally replaced the static. "Dispatch, this is Alpha One. We hear you five by five."

Applause again filled the room. Bill said, "Am I ever glad to hear your voice, Mark."

"I appreciate the love, Bill, but don't book the honeymoon just yet. I don't have time to give you the entire play by play, but our plane should be doing a data dump via satellite as we speak. We are headed to Lajes Field, and...it doesn't look like we're going to make it. Have Capt. Dale Hennessey over at the training department run some simulations and see if he has any ideas on how to extend our range. Over."

"You got it. As soon as you went missing we assembled the Accident Go Team. We'll do everything in our power to help you." He glanced at his computer monitor. Data from the plane flooded in, scrolling down the screen. "We're receiving your data now, Alpha One."

"Thanks, Bill. Oceanic, this is Alpha One. Keep the connection with dispatch open on your frequency."

Oceanic's response came over the speaker, "Roger, Alpha One, will do."

Maintenance Supervisor Russo was sitting at a computer, analyzing the data pouring in from the *Tech-Liner.* He cocked his head. "What the fuck...?

Mills looked over at Russo. "What is it?"

"This can't be right. The data musta gotten corrupted. I'm gonna rerun it." Russo tapped on his keyboard then anxiously waited.

Tech Aerospace Corporation CEO Ralph Sanders ran into the room. He grabbed Mills. "What happened? Did they find them yet?"

"We just established radio contact. We're receiving their data now."

Russo gasped. "Jeez-us!" Everyone turned toward him. "Someone on the plane hacked into the aircraft's computer network. They locked out the controls in the cockpit and diverted the plane."

Sanders immediately came to the defense of his plane, and his company's bottom line. "That's not possible. We designed the network to be impenetrable from the outside. The computers are encrypted."

Russo snapped, "Yeah, that's what the NSA said about *their* system. Look for yourself—suit!"

Sanders scanned the data. His face went ghost white.

Mills confronted Sanders. "Your plane was hijacked... by a computer?"

"Allegedly," he quickly responded.

"Allegedly, my ass," Russo fumed. "It's right here in black and white. There's a hacker on board the plane."

Mills turned to an underling standing next to him and barked, "Get the FBI in here."

Bill called the plane. "Alpha One, this is dispatch. Is there anyone else in the cockpit right now?"

Mark's voice showed his concern over the odd question. "Negative. Why?"

"There is a computer hacker or hackers aboard your plane. Somehow, they've infiltrated the plane's network. Confirm you have control of your aircraft."

"We found a Brain plugged into the master computer. That must be how they did it. As soon as we disabled it, we regained control. As far as I know...I'm in command of my plane."

CHAPTER 21

RUSSO GRABBED A mechanic next to him and pushed him toward the door. "Go to the parts department and inventory the Brain Kits. See if any are missing. Move it!"

Three stern-faced people in dark blue windbreakers emblazoned with the gold letters FBI burst into the dispatch office. Supervisory Special Agent Manuel Cortez, age fifty-one, a no-nonsense former Marine, was in charge. Built like a fireplug, he had a short, stocky body and a high-and-tight haircut. As a career agent specializing in aviation-related crimes, Cortez had seen it all. In 2015 he led the team that investigated the Germanwings Flight 9525 accident. It quickly became tragically obvious to Cortez that it was no accident. He discovered the flight, with all its innocent pax and crew, had been hijacked and intentionally crashed into a mountain by the suicidal copilot. To this day, nightmares from what he heard on the cockpit voice recorder still haunted him. The last eight minutes before slamming into the French Alps were chilling. The captain—locked out of the cockpit—could be heard in the background screaming hysterically and banging on the door.

Special Agent Terrell Hawkins, an imposing former Florida State University tight end standing six feet four, was on Cortez's right. Special Agent Martha Janik, a mere five feet two, stood on his left. She was dressed the part in a dark blue J.C. Penny pantsuit. If for some unfathomable reason she chose to wear a dress to work, she'd have no place to conceal the Glock 17 strapped to her hip. Her jacket did the job just fine. Janik's brown hair was pulled back into a severe ponytail, matching the deadly serious expression on her face. Given the choice, most men would rather face Hawkins in a dark alley than Janik. Cortez made the introductions of his team then asked, "Who's in charge?"

Mills didn't hesitate. "I am. Peter Mills. I'm the CEO." Managers in the room rolled their eyes. "I mean acting CEO, during Mr. Andrews's absence." He pointed around the room. "This is Bill. He's the dispatcher working the flight and talking to Alpha One. Ralph Sanders's company built the plane in question. Russo here is the head maintenance supervisor." With introductions completed, he asked, "What does the FBI know?"

Cortez mentally profiled the airline people before him, an occupational habit, then responded, "We've been monitoring internet traffic from ISIS, Al-Qaeda, and other terrorist groups that have made threats against airlines in the past. No one has claimed any involvement—yet. Bring me up to speed on your end."

Mills cut to the chase. "We think the plane was hijacked."

Cortez was incredulous. "How the hell did a passenger get a gun through security screening?"

"He didn't use a gun."

"He has a bomb?"

Mills stammered, "It appears...it looks like our plane was hijacked by...a laptop."

"A what?!"

Mills continued. "A hacker on board broke into the plane's computer network. But the captain believes he's back in control at this time."

"Where was the hacker taking the plane?"

Mills looked around for any help from his team. No one stepped up. Mills broke the bad news. "The middle of the Atlantic Ocean. Apparently, he was trying to run it out of fuel."

"Suicide? Son of a bitch!" Cortez turned to Janik. "Run background checks on all the passengers. Start with male foreign nationals. Then the entire crew...including the pilots. And alert the Cyber Crimes Division in DC."

"Roger that."

He turned to Hawkins. "I want the names of every person who was in that plane in the last forty-eight hours. Pull all the security camera footage from this building."

"On it."

"Who determined the plane was hacked?" Cortez asked.

"I did, Chief," Russo replied.

"Can you tell who did it?"

"Not yet. The plane is sending terabytes of data. It'll take a while. I'll handle it."

"Keep at it. I want hard evidence so we can nail the bastard that did this. You think you're up to it?"

Russo snapped his head around. In typical, cocky New Yorker lingo, he declared, "Get the fuck outta here."

A confused Cortez looked around the room. "Is that a yes?"

Everyone nodded their heads, interpreting for Russo.

"Okay, good." Cortez questioned Mills. "Has the airline received any demands for money?"

"No, not that I'm aware of. It might be a moot point. Right now, there is a good chance...it looks like they *will* be ditching."

"Jesus. Keep me informed on any new developments." Cortez pointed at Sanders. "Get all the people who programmed the computers on your plane together on a conference call. I want to talk to them."

Sanders shifted uncomfortably. "That's going to be a problem."

Cortez barked, "I don't care if you have to wake them up. Tell them it's an emergency!"

"It's not that." Sanders hesitated, then came clean. "They're all on the plane."

CHAPTER 22

SUPERVISORY SPECIAL AGENT Cortez turned to Bill. "Warn the pilots. Whoever is behind this might not be out of ideas. And tell them not to trust anyone until we figure out what the hell is going on up there."

Bill radioed the plane. "Alpha One, this is dispatch."

"Go ahead, dispatch."

"Mark, this is Bill. The FBI is on the case. They say you guys need to be on high alert up there. Be on the lookout for any suspicious behavior. And don't trust *anyone*."

DING.

Noelle looked up and saw a red light labeled COCKPIT flashing on the flight attendant panel. She hurried over and picked up the handset. "Purser."

Mark's voice blared. "Get in here. Now!"

SHE ENTERED THE cockpit wide eyed. "What's happening Mark?"

Mark didn't bother sugarcoating the bad news. He turned in his seat to face Noelle. "Dispatch said the aircraft's computers were hacked by someone on board our plane. Everything we've been seeing up here has been a lie. Everything. The hacker, or hackers, spoofed our displays, disabled satellite tracking and communication, then diverted our plane out into the middle of the ocean attempting to run it out of gas. We don't have much left, but we're trying everything we can to extend our range in hopes of making it to the Azores."

"Where?"

There was no time for a geography lesson. "Tell the crew and Andrews what's going on. Start putting everything away. Secure all loose items. And Noelle...prepare for ditching."

When her impending fate registered in Noelle's brain, her heart leaped into her throat. "Oh my God!" Practicing ditching in a warm pool at the training facility was one thing. Doing it for real, in the stormy Atlantic, in January? A cold shiver ran down the length of her spine.

Mark stood up and gently grabbed Noelle trembling shoulders. "Hey, hey, I need you. You have to hold it together for me. You can do this. This isn't your first rodeo. Remember?"

Noelle did remember.

Her expression immediately changed. She looked Mark in the eyes, defiantly crossed her arms, and said, "Obviously."

Touché!

Mark's mind flashed back to the crew briefing before leaving JFK. His face had the guilty look of a kid caught with his hand in the cookie jar. Then his expression slowly changed to a look of grudging admiration. Then an obviously deliberate boyish smile.

Noelle shook her head and rolled her eyes. *Damn him. Why does that goofy puppy dog smile of his and those irresistible green eyes always get him out of trouble with me? Damn him!* Despite her trying to stop them, the edges of Noelle's mouth curled up in a smile.

CHAPTER 23

NOELLE ENTERED THE forward galley where her crew and Andrews were huddled together. She pulled the curtain and turned to face them. They fell silent, desperate for some good news. With a stiff upper lip, Noelle spelled out the frightening predicament they faced.

This wasn't a bad 1970s disaster movie—this was the real thing.

Andrews darted out of the galley to find Hampton. The crew walked away on the verge of tears with the unmistakable look of dread written on their faces.

From the galley, Noelle and Charlotte carefully scanned the dimly lit cabin, spying on their passengers. They looked for anything suspicious. Their spy mission wasn't going to be easy. Many of the passengers were using laptops. And they all suddenly looked suspicious.

Noelle leaned over and whispered to her friend. "Charlotte, you see that guy over there?"

"The Russian?"

"Yes. Hasn't he been on his laptop the whole flight?"

"Yep, he sure has."

The sketchy-looking Russian was staring intently at his laptop.

"I'm going to see what he's up to. Wait here." Noelle slowly sauntered down the aisle trying to act nonchalant. Just as she was about to confront the Russian, the hippie chick stepped out into the aisle to put a bag in the overhead bin. Unaware she just interfered with Noelle's secret plan, she asked, "I can't get the flight progress screen to work. How much longer until we get to London?"

"Ma'am, please take your seat. The seat belt sign is on," Noelle curtly replied.

The shabbily dressed woman looked at Noelle and said, "Sure thing..." then snapped, "sky Nazi." She plopped back down in her seat with a contemptuous look of victory on her face. Noelle didn't even bother responding. She was long past being surprised by the lack of civility among airline passengers.

The element of surprise was gone. The Russian saw her coming and turned his screen away from Noelle's prying eyes. She pretended not to notice and walked slowly past, casually looking back over her shoulder to get a glimpse of what secrets the Russian was hiding. He turned the screen even farther.

She'd had enough of this cat-and-mouse game. Noelle confronted the Russian. "Sir, we're having a problem with the satellite internet connection. Do you mind if I look at your laptop?"

He closed the laptop and removed his headphones. "There is no need. My connection is satisfactory."

"It appears your laptop might be causing the problem. I need to take a look at it."

Not about to be ordered around by a mere flight attendant, the Russian barked, "I said it is fine. Go away now, *sky waitress!*"

Charlotte came up next to Noelle. "Is there a problem?"

Noelle raised her voice. "Sir, I'm going to have to insist. Give me your laptop."

Curious passengers nearby turned to watch the escalating confrontation.

"Nyet!"

"Sir, give me your laptop. Now!" Noelle ordered him.

"I told you no!"

Noelle reached over and grabbed the laptop off the tray table.

The Russian grabbed it back.

The two grown adults engaged in an embarrassing tug-of-war over the computer. Noelle finally won the contest of wills and snatched it away from the Russian.

She opened the laptop to see what secrets he was hiding. A porno movie was playing.

Noelle quickly dropped the now dirty-feeling laptop back into the embarrassed Russian's lap. "Um...I'm sorry, sir. I thought..."

Suddenly, a frantic flight attendant rushed up to scene. "Noelle, come quickly. I think the passenger in 24C is having a heart attack!"

CHAPTER 24

NOELLE AND CHARLOTTE raced to seat 24C in the darkened aft part of the cabin. Nearby passengers lifted their heads above their seats to gawk at the commotion.

A heavily perspiring, obese man was sprawled out in his seat. His panicked face was turning a sickening shade of blue.

Noelle questioned the assembled flight attendants. "What's happening?"

The flight attendant who alerted Noelle recapped. "He rang his call button, but when I asked him what he wanted he just looked at me and clutched his chest."

The woman sitting next to him pleaded, "Please help my husband. You have to do something!"

Noelle scanned the cabin. "Is there a doctor or nurse on board?"

A silver-haired gentleman with wire-rim glasses rushed up. "Can I help?"

"Are you a doctor?" Noelle asked.

"Yes. I'm Charles Day, the chief of cardiology at Mount Sinai Hospital in Manhattan." Despite his advanced age, Dr. Day looked surprisingly fit, his apparently healthy lifestyle undoubtedly motivated by treating an endless parade of stressed-out, overweight Wall Street patients in his practice. Patients who could accurately be described as heart attacks waiting to happen. Here was a doctor who actually practiced what he preached. Noelle instantly decided she could trust the man.

The woman had tears running down her face. Dr. Day calmly asked her, "Does your husband take any medications, ma'am?"

"He's supposed to take his blood pressure pill every day, but Jerry thinks he knows more than everybody, even his doctors. I nag him all the time about it but it's a waste of breath. Ever try arguing with a bull-headed lawyer, doc?

Dr. Day just shook his head.

"Tell me what you think is happening, Doctor," Noelle said.

To the trained eye it was obvious, but to be certain (and not give the lawyer, or his wife, any ammunition for a baseless malpractice lawsuit), the doctor checked the man's pulse and respiration. He declared to the assembled crowd, "This man is experiencing a full cardiac arrest. CPR needs to be started immediately."

"Move, y'all, I got this." Charlotte pushed everyone aside and ripped the man's custom-made five-hundred-dollar shirt open. She laid his seat back, laced her fingers together, one hand on top of the other, and expertly administered CPR at a hundred compressions per minute like she was trained to do every year in recurrent class (not to mention the four other times she had performed CPR during her long career). The passenger's body bounced up and down with each powerful thrust into his chest.

Noelle whipped off a lanyard around her neck with a keyring attached. She handed it to one of the flight attendants gawking at the dying man. "Get the AED and EMK!"

The flight attendant ran over to a locked overhead bin labeled CREW USE ONLY. Airliners couldn't just pull over and call an ambulance when a passenger had a serious medical issue. They all carried basic lifesaving equipment and medical supplies to help stabilize the person until the pilots could land the plane.

The nervous flight attendant fumbled with the key ring in the dark, desperately trying to find the right one. Her hands were shaking. She used her best guess and stabbed a silver key into the lock. It didn't turn.

"Hurry!" Noelle yelled.

Thankfully, the second key worked. She scooped up equipment from the bin and ran back to seat 24C.

The doctor was visibly relieved. "I hoped you had an Automatic External Defibrillator. Stop CPR." Charlotte backed off as the doctor attached two sticky pads containing electrodes to the man's chest. He placed one pad on the right center of the man's chest above the nipple and the other pad slightly below the other nipple and to the left of the ribcage. Doctor Day turned on the machine and waited. The readout on the machine slowly came to life. It showed no discernable heartbeat. Lifting the plastic cover over a red button, the doctor warned, "Clear!" He pressed the button, sending a bolt of high-voltage electricity into the man's heart. The jolt sent the large man convulsing violently upward in his seat. Doctor Day looked back at the readout on the AED.

Flatline.

He waited for the internal battery to recharge the system then zapped the man again. Spiked-shaped waveforms started scrolling across the screen, slowly growing in height. A faint, irregular beeping sound came from the AED machine. The passenger's heart had restarted.

"That's a good start, but I can't keep shocking him. What do you have in your emergency medical kit?"

Noelle handed him the kit. "I'm sorry, Doctor, we only have the basics on board. You'll have to make do with what we've got."

"There isn't much time. This man is going to die if he doesn't get to a hospital immediately."

"Doctor, the captain is doing everything he can to land as soon as possible. Can you stabilize him for now?"

"I'll do my best."

CHAPTER 25

THE IMPOSING HAWKINS burst through the door of Alpha Airline's security office, flashing his badge. "Special Agent Hawkins, FBI. I need all the security camera footage for the last forty-eight hours cued up. Now!"

The startled rent-a-cop, in his ill-fitting gray uniform, jerked his feet off the desk and dropped his sandwich. "Yes, sir. What are we looking for?" He wiped mustard from his lips with the back of his hand.

"I"—he emphasized the word—"am looking for anything out of the ordinary. Start with the hangar, followed by the parts department. Run the video through facial recognition software so I can match faces with names."

The security guard turned and looked at Hawkins in disbelief. "Are you shitting me? This is an airline, not MI6. We can't even match bags with their correct flight."

"Right...uh...then get a maintenance supervisor in here who can identify employee faces."

"You got it, G-Man."

MARK AND WALTER prepared the cockpit for the daunting challenge that lay ahead. Suddenly an alarm broke the tense silence in the cockpit. A metallic sounding, disembodied female voice, generated by the aircraft warning computer, scolded the pilots. "*Low Fuel Warning—LAND IMMEDIATELY.*" On their screens, the same message in bold red letters taunted the pilots.

Mark argued with the scolding computer voice. "Bitching Betty, unless there's a two-mile-long aircraft carrier nearby, that's not gonna happen." Never one to pass up an opportunity to get in a jab at squids, Mark added, "Can never count on the damned Navy when you need them." He looked out his window at the storm-driven waves below. "Hell, at this point I'd settle for the Hudson River."

Walter stopped his preparations and contemplated their predicament. He looked up at the center of the cockpit ceiling and said, "Carol, this is Walter. I want you to know..." He started to choke up. "It's important you know that I love you and the kids more than anything in this world. If I don't—"

Mark reached over and put his hand on his copilot's shoulder. "Walter, you don't need to do that." Mark had been a pilot long enough to know why his copilot was speaking directly into the microphone connected to the water-tight, crash-hardened cockpit voice recorder.

"Mark, you know the odds as well as I do of...Look, even if we somehow survive the ditching, we won't last long at this temperature. It's important my family knows how much I love them. This might be my last chance."

Deep down Mark knew Walter was right. The odds of surviving a ditching in stormy seas—at night, in January—were somewhere south of the odds of winning the Powerball. If the crash didn't do them in, then hypothermia certainly would.

Years ago, Mark learned firsthand about the paralyzing effects of being immersed in frigid water during Air Force Water Survival School. The memory of it sent a chill up his spine. If exposed long enough to extremely cold water, the end result was not pretty. The negative physiological responses to the cold eventually ganged up on the human body, guaranteeing drowning.

But there was one more important thing Mark learned in survival school—the will to survive can overcome almost any predicament.

Self-preservation, the strongest and most primal of all human motivations, had throughout history been responsible for incredible stories of survival. At that moment, Mark decided it was about damned time to add another story to the list.

He straightened up and declared, "We are *not* dying. Not today. No matter what it takes, we are going to reach land. You'll have all the time in the world to tell your family how much you love them after this is over, face to face."

Mark's determination seemed to perk Walter up. Still, he asked, "Aren't you scared, Mark?"

Mark refused to let his mounting fear show. *I'm the captain. I'm responsible for every person on this plane. Everyone looks to me for leadership. I have to project calm and fearlessness, no matter how I feel. Fear is not an option.*

But now, behind the locked cockpit door, it was just the two of them, pilot to pilot. Mark temporarily let down his walls. "Of course, I'm scared. But I've got a job to do. My passengers entrusted me with their lives. Don't bail on me now, Walter. I can't fly this plane solo. I need your help." Pointing to Walter's iPad, Mark asked, "Does that gizmo of yours have the approaches for Lajes Field in it—whiz kid?"

"You bet it does."

"All right then, we have a job to do. Let's get our bird on the ground."

Walter smiled and gave Mark a snappy salute. "Aye aye, Captain Smith."

Mark snapped a salute back. "We have to reduce our weight if we stand any chance of making it. Let's start by dumping all the water tanks. That's the last thing we need right now."

Walter pulled up the appropriate symbol on his screen and tapped it. Underneath the plane, water streamed out of a gray metal drain mast, instantly froze, then fell into the ocean below.

"Shut down the number one engine. That will cut our fuel burn in half."

Walter put his hand on the left engine shutoff switch. Before committing to such a critical action as shutting down an engine in flight, he vocalized his intention. "Confirm I am shutting down the left engine?"

As trained, Mark responded, "I concur. Shut down the left engine."

Walter took a deep breath then moved the switch.

THE BLOWTORCH-LIKE FLAME inside the massive GE engine extinguished. Its signature turbine engine whine went silent as the engine spooled down to a slow, steady RPM—like a gigantic pinwheel.

THE DRUNK SALESMAN ogled the flight attendants while he polished off another tiny liquor bottle. Sudden deceleration, caused by losing half the thrust propelling the plane, sent the empty bottles on his tray table tumbling to the floor. He belched. "What was that?" When he looked back out the window at the left engine, he got his answer. He reached up to the ceiling panel above his head. His first attempt at pressing the flight attendant call button went wide. On the second attempt he managed to find it. Tina walked up and pressed the call button to extinguish the light.

The salesman looked up at her with bloodshot eyes. "What the hell is going on? The engine just quit. I wanna speak to the captain."

"Calm down, sir. Let me get the purser." She waved Noelle over.

Noelle marched up. "Sir, I'm the purser on this flight. What—"

He waved her away. "I don't want to talk to you, I wanna talk to the captain."

Jan turned around and asked Noelle, "Miss, what's going on with our plane?"

The salesman turned and pointed an accusing finger at Andrews. "I heard *that guy* say the captain is trying to *kill us*. Now the engine just quit."

Noelle shot daggers at Andrews. "You son of a..." She started toward him.

He recoiled back in his seat and put both hands up, palms outward, like stop signs. "Hold on there. I never said...I think the gentleman has had a little too much to drink."

Having been in many contentious meetings with Alpha Airlines executives, hashing out favorable terms for the massive loan package from her bank, Jan said, "Don't play dumb with us, Andrews. You're the CEO of Alpha Airlines. You've been in the cockpit. The guy sitting next to him is the chairman of the board. You guys know something you're not telling us. What is it?"

The salesman pressed harder. "I demand to talk to the captain right now."

Noelle tried to calm the irate passenger. "Sir, lower your voice." Then she played dumb. "I'm sure there must be a good reason the engine was shut down."

His seatmate grabbed the salesman's upper arm. "Buddy, take it easy. Let the flight attendant find out what's going on."

He yanked his arm loose. "Don't tell me to take it easy. I wanna to talk to the captain." He stormed up the aisle toward the cockpit.

Charlotte stepped into the aisle, hands on hips, blocking his path. She looked the guy straight in the eyes and barked, "Sit down. Now!"

He glared back at her and stood his ground.

Charlotte opened a nearby overhead bin and grabbed a red halon fire extinguisher. Then she pulled the safety pin.

The salesman advanced toward Charlotte. "I'm going to the cockpit. Get out of my way."

Charlotte pointed the bell-shaped plastic nozzle toward the salesman and blasted him with a cold cloud of high-pressure white powder.

The man stopped, powder covering his face. The other passengers yelled obscenities at the drunk, telling him to sit down. Charlotte readied for another blast.

Blinded, stunned, and humiliated, the drunk wisely decided to head back to his seat, tail between his legs.

Noelle hurried over and pried the extinguisher bottle out of Charlotte's hands. "Okay, why don't you let me have that." She winked at her friend. "Thanks."

CHAPTER 26

"How's it look with one engine shut down?"

Walter typed on the keyboard and quickly got the answer. "Better. But still ditching seven miles short of the runway."

"Dammit!" Mark picked up his mic. "Oceanic, this is Alpha One. How long before the rescue ships would reach seven miles north of Lajes Field?"

Mark waited for a response. There wasn't one.

He tried again. "Oceanic, how do you read Alpha One?"

The controller answered, but a noticeable change in his tone betrayed him. "Uh...stand by, Alpha One."

IN THE DARK ATC room, the Gander Oceanic controller snuffed out his cigarette and looked up at his supervisor hovering behind him. The supervisor shrugged and shook his head in resignation.

They knew the answer to Mark's question.

The controller's hand trembled as he reluctantly keyed his mic. "Uh...Alpha One, how do you copy?"

Mark's response blared into the controller's headset, "I hear you fine. How long?" Patience was not Mark's strong suit.

"The rescue ships aren't coming, Alpha One. A squall line is moving across the area. One of the worst storms they've seen in years. The ships are already battling thirty-foot waves, and they expect conditions to get worse. The captains are saying they refuse to put their crew and ships in more danger by trying to penetrate the line of bad weather." His voice choked with emotion. "Sorry, Alpha One, you're on your own."

BOTH PILOTS' HEADS drooped.

Mark brought the mic up to his lips. "Roger." Mark lifted his thumb from the mic switch and clipped it back into its cradle.

A long silence filled the cockpit.

A DING sound shattered the silence. Mark pulled up the view from the cockpit entrance camera on the center screen. Noelle anxiously waited, with galley carts barricading the path to the door.

When he saw the picture on the screen, a craving he had successfully suppressed for over a year came roaring back. Mark's throat tightened as his mouth suddenly went dry. The liquor cart was one of the metal carts blocking the path to the cockpit. Bottles of overpriced wines and miniature versions of premium liquors covered the top of the cart.

In the past, the stresses of everyday life used to send Mark reaching for the bottle. Now his stress level was off the charts. Going cold turkey in rehab had been one of the most difficult things Mark had ever done. Denying his cravings for a drink had been a daily struggle since leaving the protective cocoon of the rehab facility. But Mark was proud he had found the inner strength to abstain from his weakness and stayed sober. And this sure as hell wouldn't be a good time to go off the wagon.

Walter looked over. "Mark? She's waiting."

Mark looked at Walter.

"What are you going to tell her?" Walter asked.

"The truth."

Mark pressed the UNLOCK button on the center console. The fortified cockpit door popped open, and Noelle quickly marched in. She bolted the door behind her.

Before Mark could speak, Noelle said, "The passengers are asking a lot of questions, Mark. We haven't told them what's really going on yet. But when you shut down the engine they knew we had a big problem."

"No sense in trying to hide our situation from them now. They deserve to know the truth. I'll make a PA explaining everything."

"Please be careful what you say. The passengers are on edge. We're close to a riot back there already."

"I'll be careful." Mark playfully added, "This isn't my first rodeo, Noelle."

She glared at Mark while simultaneously flashing a reluctant smile. "Very funny. What about the flight map? They're asking about it."

"I'll turn it back on."

Noelle nodded and turned to leave.

Mark grabbed her arm. "Noelle..."

She turned back.

He took a deep breath. "The rescue ships aren't coming. Their captains don't think it's safe to try to penetrate the bad weather. I would've made the same call if it was me. If we ditch, nobody is coming to rescue us."

Noelle's head dropped. She tightly closed her eyes, wishing this was all just a bad dream.

Mark took her hand, trying to comfort her. "Look, I've never been any good at expressing my feelings. You know that better than anybody. But I need to tell you something else."

Noelle kept her eyes tightly shut.

He decided it was time to tell Noelle the real truth. Mark drew in a deep breath. "Noelle, please open your eyes."

When she did, her crystal-blue eyes they were filled with tears.

The sight of her tears acted like an invisible key, causing a part of himself kept deeply hidden to suddenly pop open like a sprung lock. Mark bared his soul. "God knows I've made a lot of mistakes in my life, Noelle. A lot. And I know it's a little late, but...I'm sorry I hurt you. I've been a real jerk. You and Mary deserved better. Can you ever forgive me?"

Noelle put her hand on Mark's and looked into his green eyes. She saw eyes full of pain. Mark's face looked like it had aged a decade since taking off at JFK. Despite the brave front he was putting up, Noelle knew him well enough to see the incredible stress he was under. She bravely said, "Let's not worry about the past right now. There will be plenty of time to talk later. You concentrate on finding a way to get us down safely, okay?"

"I won't let you down, Noelle. We *will* make it to the airport."

Doing her best to make the lie sound convincing, Noelle said, "I know we will. I trust you." She bent down and softly kissed Mark goodbye on the cheek. Her lips brushed his ear. Noelle whispered, "I've always loved you, Mark. It's important you know that."

A wisp of hair fell across her forehead. Mark instinctively reached up and brushed it back in place. Mark's eyes moistened. He wanted to tell Noelle so much more, but the words escaped him.

Noelle saw the pain written on Mark's face from years of regret. *Why did it have to end like this? After all we've been through. Why didn't we just put aside our stubborn pride and work things out?* The pain of regret was now mirrored on Noelle's face.

She stood up, straightened her skirt, and wiped the tears from her eyes. "I've got to get the cabin ready." She spun around and left the cockpit.

For the first time that night, Mark noticed the fragrant, enticing scent of her perfume. Would this be the last?

NOELLE STOOD RESOLUTELY at the flight attendant panel in the front of the cabin.

Mark's voice came over the PA, "Ladies and gentlemen, this is your captain speaking. I need everyone's undivided attention." As soon as the passengers heard the nervous tone in his voice, the cabin fell silent. "We've experienced a very serious problem with our navigation system, requiring us to divert to the Azores. Unfortunately, that has put us critically short on fuel. There is a possibility we might have to ditch the airplane."

The salesman looked up. "Did he say ditch? In the ocean?"

Noelle turned on the large flight progress screen at the front of the cabin. Passengers squinted to examine it. Their eyes widened with every passing second.

The situation it depicted was terrifying. The course line abruptly ended in the Atlantic Ocean, north of the Azores.

The salesman elbowed his seatmate. "We're dead." He unscrewed the top from another small bottle and downed its contents in one gulp.

Mark continued. "I'm asking everyone to remain calm and follow the instructions of your flight attendants. Rest assured we're doing everything we can up here to get you on the ground safely. We'll be starting down soon. I expect it to be a little bumpy during our descent, so please remain seated. Thank you." Short, sweet, and to the point.

As comprehension of what they were facing dawned on the passengers, panic erupted in the cabin. They yelled questions at the flight attendants, demanding answers. People paced the aisles, which only served to reinforce the certainty there was no escape from their predicament. Every passenger's unspoken nightmare had just become a reality for the people trapped on the Tech-Liner.

So much for not panicking the passengers.

Noelle picked up her PA microphone. "Everyone, please give me your full attention. Stow any loose items around you at this time. Pull out the safety information card in the seat-back pocket in front of you, and thoroughly review the instructions for ditching. Don your life vests now, but *do not inflate them*. If you need any assistance, let one of us know. Also, if the plane remains intact after ditching, I need four able-bodied volunteers per raft to retrieve the life rafts from the closets." Not surprisingly, no one raised their hand to volunteer for the job of staying behind to lug two-hundred-pound rafts inside a sinking airplane.

The shocked passengers slowly began to follow Noelle's instructions. As the severity of their situation hit home, passengers pulled out their smartphones and opened their laptops.

The life vests could wait.

DETERMINED TO STAY at their fuel-efficient altitude as long as possible, Mark focused on the readout on the screen in front of himself. He watched the miles remaining until the Top of Descent (TOD) point slowly tick down toward zero. To his amazement, the countdown seemed to be slowing down, each mile taking longer to fly than the last. "Dammit, the winds have shifted to a headwind." Finally, the number on the screen grudgingly rolled over to zero. *Okay, here we go.* "We're at top of descent," Mark told Walter. "Go ahead and start down. Fly at green dot airspeed to maximize our range. And for God's sake, don't turn on the autopilot."

"Green dot and ignore George. You got it, boss."

As the plane nosed over, the angry sea below filled the view out of every window.

CHAPTER 27

RALPH SANDERS, ALPHA'S COO Peter Mills, and others congregated in a break room close to the dispatch office, anxiously watching multiple TVs. The words BREAKING NEWS splayed across every screen, accompanied by jolting synthesized music. Nonstop coverage on the disappearance of the Tech-Liner played on every channel. Anchors on the twenty-four-hour news channels were salivating at the prospect of a real-life disaster. They realized the story could lead each thirty-minute regurgitation of the day's headlines for at least a full week; or until the next celebrity cheating scandal knocked it off its perch.

A blonde reporter, trying her best to appear genuinely concerned, read a hastily prepared script off the teleprompter. "Information is starting to trickle in about the fate of Flight Alpha One. The plane has one hundred passengers and ten crew members aboard. More than four hours after vanishing, we now know they are attempting a very dangerous maneuver—landing during a storm on a tiny island in the Azores, in the middle of the Atlantic Ocean. Oddly, the island chain is thousands of miles from their original destination of London, England. How could the newest airliner in the world go off course so badly? Do they have enough fuel to reach the tiny island? We'll ask our own aviation reporter Nick Fields those questions after these important messages." The screen switched to a McDonald's commercial.

Mills looked over at Sanders. "This is a nightmare. And the whole world is watching it."

"It's a nightmare, all right."

Mills glared at Sanders. "You mean for those poor people on the plane, right?"

"Yes...of course. Yes."

Mills rolled his eyes and turned his attention to another TV.

A redheaded anchor was handed a note from off screen. She looked sideways at her producer for guidance. Getting none, she read the note. "As we await additional details on Flight Alpha One, something unprecedented is happening. Trapped aboard a doomed airliner and helpless to change their fate, passengers are communicating with loved ones using the plane's satellite Wi-Fi network. Facebook, YouTube, and Twitter are experiencing sporadic outages from record levels of traffic as the entire world joins in to follow the unfolding tragedy in real time."

An airline supervisor rushed into the breakroom and grabbed Mills. "Mr. Mills, I just talked to the head of reservations. His system is crashing"—he winced inside at his poor choice of words—"and every phone line he has is swamped with calls from frantic family and friends. What do I tell him?"

"Tell him the reservation agents are not to tell anyone anything. The media is all over this. We can't afford to be seen giving out incorrect information. PR has activated the emergency 800 number for families to call. I just recorded the standard response script for it."

"Standard response?"

"You know, 'We understand this is a very difficult situation for the families of our passengers...as soon as we have updates we will pass them along...we're doing everything we can.' The standard script."

THE FLIGHT ATTENDANTS tried to get the passengers ready for ditching, but they had more important concerns. Passengers struggled to compose final messages that would adequately convey a lifetime of feelings to their loved ones.

A young Englishman typed an email on his laptop while silently crying. It read: "My dearest Elizabeth. It looks like I'll be a little late for our wedding. Please keep a stiff upper lip whilst you wait to hear from me. Yours Always, Nigel."

Jan Frey recorded a video on her smartphone as she sobbed uncontrollably. "Mommy loves you guys so, so much. Please be good for Daddy, okay? Tom, you are my soul mate. I'm so sorry about our fight last night. I didn't mean what I said."

CAPT. DALE HENNESSEY, cocky ex-fighter jock and chief instructor for Alpha Airlines, appeared at the doorway of the break-room. He motioned to Mills to step out into the hallway. When Mills did, Hennessey pointed toward the fire exit. The pair looked around then walked silently to the end of the hallway. Convinced they hadn't been seen, they stepped into the fire exit stairwell.

"Well?" Mills asked.

Hennessey shook his head. "Sorry, Mr. Mills. I tried every possible trick I could think of in the simulator. I crunched the numbers myself. They aren't going to make it."

Mills started pacing. "There's got to be something else you can try. Something you missed?"

Offended, Hennessey's outsize ego kicked in. "I did not *miss* anything, Mr. Mills. Mark is a friend of mine. I'm positive if there was any way to extend his plane's range, I would have found it."

"Dammit!" Mills punched the fire-rated steel door. He glared at Hennessey. "What am I supposed to tell the families? Sorry I couldn't figure out a way for your kid to not die. My bad. Do you realize the shit storm that will create for me? The press will have a field day."

The offended look on Hennessey's face changed. He perceived an opportunity. "Only if they find out about it."

Mills narrowed his gaze. "What are you saying, Captain Hennessey?"

"What I'm saying, is..."—he looked Mills in the eyes—"tragically, the airline is going to need a new CEO after today." Seeing the comprehension he was hoping for, Hennessey played his hand. "And a new chief pilot."

Without saying another word, the two men shook hands. Everything that needed to be said was said.

WALTER CHECKED THE computer again then broke the bad news. "We aren't going to make it, Mark. We're still too heavy."

Mark's back was against the wall. "I'll be damned if I'm going to be remembered forever as the second Captain Smith to go down in the Atlantic."

A mischievous grin crossed Mark's face. "Close the pressurization isolation valve for the aft cargo compartment."

Walter looked suspiciously at Mark. "Come again?"

"Close the valve, Walter."

Walter tapped a symbol on his screen. It turned red. "Okay, it's isolated."

"Vent the residual pressure in the compartment. We're about to lighten our load."

Walter gasped. "Open the cargo door? In flight? Surely, you can't be serious?"

"Yes, Walter, yes I am. Vent the pressure."

"I hope this is a good idea."

A SMALL FLAP in the middle of the aft cargo door opened. Warm, pressurized air streamed out of the vent flap, creating a loud hiss. When the warm inside air met the frigid outside air, it immediately condensed, creating a thin white contrail of ice crystals down the right side of the plane.

Hearing the hissing sound, Andrews sat up straight and looked around. He jumped up and ran to a window on the right side. When he looked back and saw the contrail, Andrews sprinted to the front of the cabin.

Noelle stood guard in front of galley carts blocking access to the cockpit. Andrews waved his chubby finger at her and ordered, "Get out of my way. I'm going in the cockpit."

Furious at Andrews for his betrayal of Mark, Noelle stood her ground. "After what you accused Mark of? Like hell you are."

"I'm warning you, bitch. Move! Now!"

Noelle didn't move an inch, returning Andrews's disdainful look.

"I'm warning you."

She stood her ground, chin held high.

Andrews reared back with his right arm, fist balled up tight. Before he could start it forward to take a swing at Noelle, his arm froze.

Charlotte had a vise-like hold of Andrews's right wrist. She rotated his arm in ways it wasn't meant to rotate. Andrews's knees buckled from the pain. Charlotte calmly asked Noelle, "Is there a problem, honey?"

"Mr. Andrews was just asking my permission to use the intercom to call the cockpit. Isn't that right, Mr. Andrews?"

He glared at her and refused to answer.

"I don't think you want to tangle with my best friend," Noelle warned.

Charlotte twisted even harder.

Andrews winced in pain. "Okay! Okay! If it isn't too much of a bother, Ms. Parker, could I use your intercom to call the cockpit?"

"Didn't you forget the magic word?"

"Please?"

"Why certainly, Mr. Andrews. Be my guest."

Charlotte reluctantly released his wrist then stood guard next to Noelle.

Andrews rubbed his right wrist for a few seconds to get the circulation going again. He picked up the intercom handset with his left hand and pushed the COCKPIT button.

MARK PICKED UP.

"Smith, this is Andrews! Don't you dare open the cargo door! You'll kill us all!"

Mark was not about to engage in a debate with the man who had vetoed his request for extra fuel. "Andrews, I have two choices: do nothing and guarantee we will be ditching without any chance of rescue or roll the dice and hope for the best. Either way, this is what I get paid the big bucks to do—take calculated risks in life-threatening situations. If I didn't have the balls to make tough calls when it counted, then I'd be...I guess I'd be you. If you don't like it, fire me!"

Andrews face turned beet red. He bellowed, "I should have done that years ago! You're fired, Smith!"

Mark slammed the handset down. He said, "I've got the aircraft." Walter released his stick. Mark took control of the jet, took a deep breath, and tapped the symbol on his screen labeled AFT CARGO DOOR. Mark then turned on all the exterior lights on the plane. He and Walter watched the door open on the tail camera feed. Assisted by the wind, the cargo door rapidly swung open.

THERE WAS NOW a 10'x10' hole in the side of the plane.

A loud roar filled the passenger cabin as air blasted past the open compartment at over three times the speed of a raging Category 5 hurricane. Curious passengers flocked to the right side of the plane, pressing their noses to the windows. They watched in horror as their expensive checked luggage spewed out of the open door.

As the bags left, they ricocheted off the Saudi Prince's gleaming Rolls Royce, denting the sheet metal and shattering windows. The powerful suction created by the passing air pulled the massive car toward the opening. It inched forward on the cargo pallet, causing the braided nylon straps holding down the car to groan under the strain. The strap across the hood quickly reached the limit of its tensile strength and snapped. Then the trunk strap broke. Finally, the long front-to-back strap surrendered. The silver Ghost shot nose first out of the cargo compartment in a flash. It tumbled end over end, eventually reaching terminal velocity on its way to a watery grave. When it hit the icy water, the Rolls Royce exploded into 450,000 expensive pieces.

His face bright red, Basara shrieked, "My Rolls!" One of his wives jumped up, pulled off her hijab, and threw it down at the feet of Basara. "For once, quit your bitching. You have fifteen more just like it."

THE PLANE SUDDENLY started to buck and weave through the night sky. Passengers out of their seats were tossed about like rag dolls. Some landed with a thud in the aisle, some in the laps of seated passengers. Those buckled in felt like they were being crushed down in their seats by the positive g-forces. Moments later they were forcefully levitated toward the ceiling as the g's went negative, held down only by the thin strap of their seatbelts. Mark tried to smooth out the violent oscillations, but his control-stick movements weren't effective. His pulse spiked as he yelled, "I can't control the plane! The computer's fighting me!"

The computerized fly-by-wire flight control system was in uncharted territory. It had never been programmed to handle this type of scenario. The system had no way of knowing the aft cargo compartment was suddenly empty of all its weight, drastically shifting the plane's center of gravity forward. Or that the open cargo door was radically disrupting the aerodynamics. Its designers never dreamed of programming the flight control computer to handle such an abnormal combination. And the computer, not the pilot, had the final say on how and when the flight controls moved. The computer normally evaluated the pilot's stick movements, compared them to a known set of flight regimes, and then sent a signal to move the appropriate flight controls. The result was a smooth ride that passengers wouldn't notice. But "normal" and this flight were two things that didn't belong in the same sentence. The open cargo door disrupted the airflow as it traveled back over the tail, causing it to flutter. The computer didn't know why and started acting irrationally, sending random movement signals to various flight controls.

Mark quickly reached out and tapped the symbol on the screen to close the cargo door. The door symbol turned red and started to blink. He tapped the symbol again. Nothing changed. Mark pointed at the view from the tail camera. "We've got a bigger problem. The door won't close."

"The air load on the door must be too great. The hydraulic actuators can't overcome it." Walter pulled up the schematic of the plane's hydraulic system on his screen. "The hydraulic pressure is in the danger zone. The actuators will keep pulling until they rip themselves off the door."

"Shut off pressure. Freeze the actuators. If they fail, the door will never close."

Walter shut off pressure to the hydraulic actuators. "Okay, the pressure is returning to normal. Now what?"

"The only way to reduce the air load is to slow down." Mark rolled his neck and shoulders to release built-up tension. "Here we go." He pulled the throttle for the right engine back to idle. The airspeed started rapidly dropping.

THE SOUND IN the cabin dropped from a roar to an eerie quiet as the plane slowed. The poor passengers mistakenly assumed the second engine had now quit. Screaming broke out once again.

MARK ATTEMPTED TO fly the combative plane at the edge of a stall to minimize the air load on the door. "Try it again."

Walter turned the hydraulic pressure to the door actuators back on. "All right, pressure is normal. The door is closing."

Halfway closed, the door suddenly stopped. The red door symbol on the screen started blinking.

"The door stopped again. You have to fly slower."

"I can't! We go any slower and we'll fall out of the sky."

"Hydraulic pressure is spiking again. I've got to shut it off," Walter warned.

"No, wait! Give it a few more seconds."

The hydraulic pressure blasted past the red line. The pilots nervously waited. Their eyes darted back and forth between the door symbol and the rising hydraulic pressure. The pressure continued higher. The door symbol remained red.

"Mark, I have to shut it off," Walter pleaded.

"Just a few more..."

The symbol on the screen finally changed from red to green. The door was safely closed and locked. The flight control computer now had a scenario it could handle, and the ride smoothed out.

Mark breathed a deep sigh of relief. His gamble had paid off. He pushed the right engine throttle lever back to full power then gladly returned the flying duties to Walter. "You've got the plane. How's it look now?"

Walter punched buttons on the keypad. He was elated. "Yes! That helped a lot. Assuming nothing else goes wrong, we'll be short by only two miles now."

Mark shook his head. "Not good enough. Two miles out to sea might as well be twenty. Still means we'll be ditching."

CHAPTER 28

DESPITE THE THREATENINGLY titled FAA regulation—*Title 14 Code of Federal Regulations, part 121.306 - Subject: Passenger Compliance with Crewmember Safety Instructions Regarding the Use of Portable Electronic Devices (PED)*—the passengers aboard the Tech-Liner didn't seem too worried about it. Passengers with smartphones and tablets violated the regulation with abandon.

No one aboard the plane prepared for ditching despite the constant pleadings of the flight attendants. In the chaos, Noelle noticed the doctor who'd attended to the heart attack victim walking solemnly up the aisle. When he saw her, Doctor Day stopped and silently shook his head—admission, despite his impressive credentials, there was nothing more he could have done.

The last thing Mark needed was this tragic development added to his already overburdened plate. Noelle decided any news that could potentially distract Mark from getting them to dry land was not going to be passed up to the cockpit by her, or anyone else.

In the lounge, Hampton was finally acting like the chairman of the board. "Andrews, you bullied the board into signing off on this damned plane. Now not only is *it* going down; you will have brought down the *entire airline*. Then you tried to blame Smith for all of this. His quick thinking might have saved us. Then I find out from the Purser you refused his request for more fuel, and that you just *fired* Captain Smith?"

Andrews tried to shift blame once more. "Tech Aero is the bad guy here, not me. And don't forget the FAA. If they had done their jobs right, none of this would have happened."

That was the last straw for Hampton. "You sniveling little weasel. I should have known better than to hire outside the Ivy League. You're the one that's fired!"

Noelle walked toward the front of the cabin when suddenly she heard a loud *POP!* Then a second *POP!* Followed by a third and fourth in rapid succession. She turned toward the noise. A few panicked passengers had decided to ignore her earlier instructions. They were inflating their life vests *inside the plane*. Noelle grabbed the PA mic. “Stop! Stop! Do *not* inflate your life vests yet. Wait until you get outside the plane. If it fills with water, you will be pinned to the ceiling and drown.” The prospect of being trapped inside a sinking airplane by the very device that was supposed to keep you from drowning immediately stopped any additional activations.

IN THE BREAK room next to dispatch, the growing crowd watched a report from a suitably serious-looking brunette anchor. “In a heart-wrenching example of the pervasiveness of social media in our lives, passengers of the doomed flight are uploading live video to YouTube as they face an unimaginable situation. Video from “Marvin 69” shows the aircraft apparently starting to break apart in flight. Roll the video.”

Video from a passenger smartphone, shot through a window on the Tech-Liner, started. It showed the cargo door opening, followed by objects flashing out of frame. At the end of the video, Marvin 69 turned the phone around and mugged for the camera.

With the camera back on her, the reporter added an intentionally frightening comment: “How much longer the crippled plane can stay together is anyone’s guess.” She held her finger up to her earpiece and nodded. “Okay, I’m being told our news crews have just arrived in Brooklyn.

They are at the home of the parents of one of the passengers on the plane. Let's go there live."

LIKE PIRANHA, A news crew stalked a middle-aged couple as they walked hurriedly up their driveway, smartphones in hand. A bright light mounted on top of the shoulder-carried camera illuminated its prey. The reporter shoved a microphone in the woman's face. "I understand your son is on the plane. How are you feeling right now?"

The wife was sobbing uncontrollably. "He's our only child. I feel so helpless. There's nothing we can do to save him. It's tearing my heart out."

The husband turned and violently shoved the lens of the camera. "Get that damned thing out of our faces!"

The feed from the camera abruptly turned to static.

BACK IN THE break room a woman broke down crying and fled the room. The others in the room wanted to comfort her but felt helpless themselves.

THE ANCHOR IN the station was back live. Normally an emotional vampire who lived for a tragedy like this one, she was caught momentarily speechless at the callousness of their on-sight news crew. She looked off camera for help. The crew behind the cameras just shrugged. Her words stumbled out, "Uh...that report...Jimmy, do we need to take a commercial break? No? Okay, moving on..."

The rattled anchor was relieved to have the scrolling script on the teleprompter to fall back on. "Because of technology, we now have the unprecedented ability to watch tragic events unfold live. Imagine being on the Titanic, but this time with internet access. What would your final message to loved ones say? This gruesome new ability has some in the social media community questioning the ethical boundaries of the medium. Has technology gone too far?" She put down the blank stack of papers in her hand and pretended to reflect. "How about *our* role in sensationalizing situations like this? Don't *we* deserve some blame?" She winced as something was yelled in her earpiece. "Okay, I guess we're cutting to a commercial now."

MARY SMITH STROLLED through the Duke University student union carrying a stack of thick medical text books under her arm. A large group had huddled around a TV hung from the wall, nervously watching. As she walked by the crowd, Mary heard a reporter on the television say the doomed flight was under the command of Capt. Mark Smith.

Mary froze in her tracks and snapped her head toward the TV. Her focus was drawn to the text of a news ticker crawling right to left along the bottom of the screen: LONDON FLIGHT LOST AT SEA! She pushed bodies left and right, forcing her way through the crowd to get a closer look. Her blue eyes locked on to the screen. Pictures of the entire crew, with names under each, flashed on the screen. In a loud gasp, air expelled from Mary's lungs as if Mike Tyson just landed an uppercut to her solar plexus. Her vision narrowed. The crowd around her disappeared from her consciousness. All she could think about was how she always had something more important to do than calling her mom to chat, and the terrible way she treated her dad only a few hours earlier. Her textbooks spilled to the floor as she ran off crying.

CHAPTER 29

THE PRESS BRIEFING room at FAA Headquarters in Washington DC was packed wall to wall with cameras, producers, and reporters.

Administrator Hernandez nervously rocked back and forth at a podium bristling with news outlet microphones. He was visibly sweating. Salivating reporters peppered him with inane questions.

He repeated his non-answer for the fifth time. "As I said before, we are still gathering the facts about Flight Alpha One at this time. We will have an update for you as soon as we know more." Hernandez pointed to a waving reporter. "You, in the back."

"Thank you, Administrator. Ben Sizemoore, aviation beat reporter with the *Wall Street Journal.* Two questions. Is it true you were supposed to be on the flight?" With concern in his voice he asked, "If so, what happened?"

"Yes, I was. But I was called back to my office at the last minute by my staff on a pressing matter unrelated to this incident." His aides looked at each other with puzzled expressions, having just been thrown under the bus.

With his victim properly set up, the reporter went in for the kill (minus the concern in his voice). "My second question, Administrator Hernandez. Are you aware my paper did a series of articles one year ago about the issue of cybersecurity and the threat hackers pose to modern jetliners?"

Hernandez squirmed and avoided eye contact with the reporter. "I don't believe I recall the article." Typical lawyer answer.

Sizemoore grinned like the Cheshire Cat. "Let me refresh your memory. After the articles came out, you said, and I quote, 'Current FAA certification standards ensure aircraft computers are impenetrable from hackers. The safety of the flying public is always our top priority here at the FAA. Therefore, I see no need to burden the aircraft manufacturers with unnecessary and costly new regulations', end quote." Sizemoore then went for the jugular. "Care to address the flying public on the wisdom of your decision—in light of the current situation?"

Hernandez looked over to his staff for help. They looked down at their Blackberrys, having no intention of bailing him out. "I...well, you see...Uh, let me..."

Barry Eisman, FAA chief legal counsel, jumped in front of the podium with his arms raised up high, shielding Hernandez from the flashing cameras. "No more questions. The administrator will be happy to answer any other questions you have at our next briefing." He whisked the befuddled political appointee off the stage.

Reporters rushed toward Hernandez like rabid wolves that smelled blood.

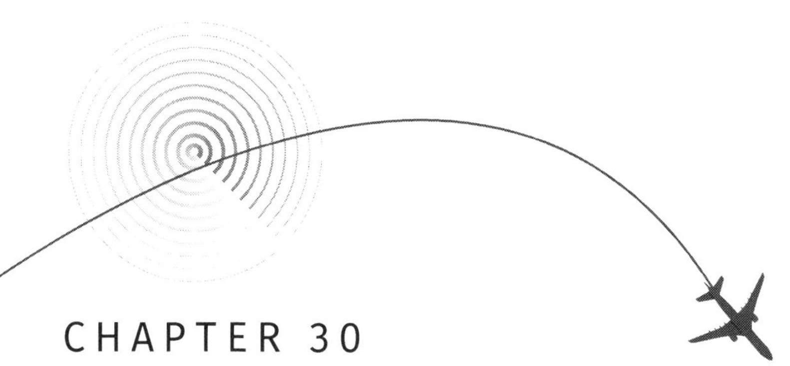

CHAPTER 30

AS THE PLANE approached the Azores, the night sky was enveloped by thick storm clouds from the squall line. Turbulence jostled the plane left and right as it plowed through the clouds. Large raindrops sounded like BBs bouncing off the two-inch-thick windshield.

The sound of the rain brought Mark's mind back to a frightening flight from his past. He had been a green second lieutenant in the Air Force. Young, dumb, and thinking he was invincible, Mark had painted himself into a corner by pushing the fuel on a solo cross-country flight in the T-38 Talon. The sleek, supersonic trainer was appropriately nicknamed the "White Rocket." Now

Mark's rocket was in danger of flaming out and falling to earth.

During his time in the Air Force, Mark had seen how random fate could be. He'd known good pilots who'd died through no fault of their own. They just happened to be in the wrong place at the wrong time. Mark wished he could blame fate for the jam he was in back then, but it was his own fault. Flying on fumes with no alternate airports within reach, Mark had to choose between two bad options: land at England Air Force Base in Alexandria, Louisiana with a tornado closing in on the field or eject over a populated city if his jet flamed out. He did a quick sign of the cross and decided to try landing.

The ride was so violent it felt like being strapped to one of those mechanical bulls popular in country bars. Luckily, the plane had held together, and Mark was on course, because he had caught sight of the runway one second before the plane slammed down hard on it.

He'd challenged the awesome power of Mother Nature and survived. But she was a harsh mistress when it came to foolish aviators. Rarely did pilots best her twice and live to tell about it. The experience didn't dent Mark's love of flying, but he was never so happy to be on solid ground.

Now, decades later, fate appeared coiled up and ready to strike again. Unfortunately for his passengers and crew, they happened to be in the wrong place at the wrong time.

The voice of the Gander Oceanic controller broke in over the cockpit speaker. "Alpha One, this is Oceanic, how do you copy?"

The call jolted Mark back to his predicament. He grabbed the mic from its cradle. "Go ahead, Oceanic."

"I have the weather at Lajes. Not good. Visibility is going down fast at the airport due to heavy rain. If...*when* you reach the airport, the weather will be well below landing minimums."

As Mark started to respond, the plane was jolted so hard by turbulence that it knocked the microphone out of his hand. Mark shook his head, picked up the mic, and uttered the minimum response, "Roger." He reasoned, *why bother engaging in a conversation with Gander about the weather—it won't change it.*

Mark turned to Walter. "Got any ideas?"

His head drooped low as if in surrender. "I wish I did, Mark. I'm afraid we're all out of tricks. It's over," Walter lamented. "I guess my family won't be needing a bigger car after all."

Mark's head cocked to the side. "What kind of car did Mo sell you?"

"Chevy Suburban. A real land yacht. Big enough to fit four car seats and two dogs. Perfect for us. As long as there is a gas station every other block."

"You run the air conditioner much when you drive?"

"In Florida? Nonstop. Especially with a wife pregnant out to here." Walter exaggerated by reaching his right hand out to full arm's length. "Why?"

Mark's seafoam-green eyes showed renewed hope for the first time in hours. "Close the bleed air valve on engine number two."

Walter smiled like a kid at Christmas. "Well, *I'll be damned.* Yes, sir!" He tapped his screen, pulling up a systems diagram for the engine, then tapped the green ENG #2 BLEED AIR VALVE symbol. The symbol rotated ninety degrees then turned red.

During flight, some of the clean heated air from jet engines is diverted into the plane. Similar to how running A/C in a car reduces gas mileage, drawing (bleeding) hot air off a jet engine reduces a plane's range slightly. Normally, that's not a problem. Unless of course you're going to be two miles short of the only runway within thousands of miles. In a last-ditch effort to squeeze out a few more minutes of operation from the remaining engine, Mark decided to turn off the heat.

The problem is, without heat, the air inside would eventually cool to the same subarctic temperature of the air outside the plane's thin aluminum skin. Obviously, this wasn't going to go over too well with the passengers. They preferred the ice be in their drinks, not in their veins.

The only way to find warmer outside air was to fly at a much lower altitude—which greatly increases fuel consumption. Fuel they didn't have. Rock, meet hard place.

"You know what this means, don't you?"

"It means we better put our jackets on," Mark dryly replied.

Mark unbuckled and walked over to the coat closet. He handed Walter his dark blue uniform jacket with three gold stripes on the sleeve. Walter buttoned every button after slipping it on. He looked at his own jacket solemnly draped over Mo.

Mark stroked his chin, narrowed his gaze, then decided to leave it right where it was. The dead man's jacket would have to do.

He pulled Mo's jacket from the closet. Before Mark could force the smaller man's jacket over his broad shoulders, it split all the way down the back seam. Disgusted, Mark wiggled out of the destroyed jacket and threw it back in the closet. He turned back toward Mo. With an embarrassed expression, Mark said, "Sorry, Mo, I'm going to need this more than you will." Mark carefully lifted his jacket and slipped it on.

Mo didn't appear to mind.

CHAPTER 31

AGENT JANIK WAS seated at a gray metal desk in an Alpha Airlines office. She had commandeered the room for use as a temporary FBI tactical command post. No airline personnel had dared tell her no. Agent Hawkins hovered nearby.

Janik was sitting at attention, engaged in an animated call on her cell phone. "Yes, sir; that's correct, sir. Two agents from our Madrid legal attaché office are on a Gulfstream. They're headed to the Azores to assist our guys already on site. A mechanic; that's correct, sir. We nabbed him as he was boarding a flight out of the country. They're bringing him in now." She listened for a moment then sat up even straighter. "Thank you, sir. It was a team effort." Janik gave Hawkins a thumbs-up. "We will, sir. Thank you, sir." After she hung up, a smile crossed Janik's face for the first time that night.

Mills poked his head into the room with an update. "We're still analyzing the data. Nothing definitive yet. Any progress on your end?"

"We got the bastard! He's one of your mechanics," Janik boasted.

Mills gulped. "One of *our guys* did this?"

Supervisory Special Agent Cortez burst through the door, leading Ahmed Harris into the office in handcuffs. He pushed Ahmed down hard into a chair. "Sit down, you son of a bitch."

Ahmed scowled at the agents, looking scared but defiant.

Cortez took a deep breath. Regaining his composure, he started the interrogation. "Security cameras filmed you walking into the parts department with a backpack in the middle of the night two days ago. Now we find this..."

Hawkins thumped a gray metal case labeled CONTROLLED ITEM, BRAIN KIT #3 onto the desk. He wore latex gloves to not contaminate any fingerprints on what could be Exhibit No. 1 during the trial. He opened the case. The cutouts in the protective foam were empty.

Cortez continued the grilling. "What did you do with the Brain that was in that case, Ahmed? Swap it with the one you were supposed to use during the aircraft preflight tests? No, you look too stupid to have thought that up. Maybe your accomplices did? Who else is in on this with you?"

Ahmed ignored his questions.

"You better start talking, Ahmed."

Ahmed stared straight ahead, trying to suppress any micro expressions that would betray his fear—unaware his body tells had long ago betrayed the macho persona he tried to project.

Making no headway, Cortez tried the good cop approach. "Look, we know it was you, Ahmed. If you come clean and tell me everything, I'll consider recommending to the DOJ that capital punishment be taken off the table. Frying in the electric chair is a horrible way to go, Son."

Ahmed sat stone-faced.

Cortez pointed to the empty case. "Forensics just dusted the case for prints. Whose fingerprints do you think they'll find on it? If you screwed up and left even a partial print on it, we gotcha. You know that, right?"

Ahmed leaned forward and glared at Cortez with dark, soulless eyes. "Go to hell, Cortez. You don't have squat."

Cortez started to reel him in. "Maybe, for now. But we know you have accomplices on the plane. We'll figure out who they are. And once we do, they'll flip on you in a second."

"Bullshit."

"Oh, they'll rat you out, all right. Rats always find a way to save their own asses when cornered, don't they? Once we inform them that they're facing the death penalty, you can bet one of them will suddenly decide to cooperate. That is, of course, if the plane makes it to the Azores and they survive. If not, we'll tack their deaths on to the counts you're already facing."

"You're bluffing."

"You think so, tough guy. And why is that?" Cortez delivered the innocuous-sounding question with such skill that his comrades nodded with admiration—then waited.

Ahmed sat back in his chair and smirked. "Because you're FBI, that's why. She knows you have no jurisdiction in the Azores. Go fuck yourself."

The three agents looked at each other and smiled, collectively thinking, *Amateur.*

Cortez told Janik, "There's only one hacker—a female. Run the background checks again. Only female passengers this time."

Ahmed's head sank.

MARY BURST INTO her dorm room and locked the door behind her. She stood with her back pressed against the door, immobilized by guilt. The thought of both her parents perishing at the same time in a plane crash a million miles away was overwhelming. Breathing became impossible. Mary covered her eyes with her palms and pushed her head back against the door. *Think. Think. How can I contact them?* With parents who were at least three steps behind old-school, using the high-tech apps Mary and her friends used to communicate wasn't a viable option. She held back tears as she dialed her iPhone. When it connected she heard: "*Hi. You've reached Noelle Parker. Sorry I can't take your call. I must be flying to some exotic destination. Leave a message after the...*" Mary stabbed the phone icon in frustration. She quickly dialed again. After listening to the message and the beep, she said, "Daddy, it's me..."

CHAPTER 32

RELENTLESSLY BURNING PRECIOUS fuel, the plane descended lower and lower toward the frigid, merciless sea. The growing feeling of dread among the passengers made the spacious cabin feel more like a claustrophobic death-row prison cell with no hope of escape.

People looked around at their fellow passengers for signs others were experiencing similar emotions as they faced their impending demise. At some point in life, most people wondered how they would act in a true life-or-death situation. Would they act no better than a wild animal, proving Darwin right, or like an intelligent, courageous human being? Soon enough, the passengers aboard the world's newest airline would have an answer to that question.

Noelle had the intercom handset up to her ear. Mark explained the reason for the rapid drop in temperature in the cabin, then said, "I'm afraid it's going to get very cold. There's nothing I can do about it. I did it to save gas. Do whatever you can to keep the crew and passengers warm."

Noelle hung up, cleared her throat, then made a PA announcement. "Ladies and gentlemen, I know a lot of you are asking about the cold temperature in the cabin. Unfortunately, the captain has just informed me that the heat will remain off the rest of the flight. If you have a jacket, please retrieve it and put it on. If not, wrap yourself tightly in your duvet like a sleeping bag."

Few passengers had the foresight to bring a jacket with them adequate to handle subzero temperatures. The ones that had, quickly put them on to ward off the cold. The remaining passengers wrapped up like mummies in their high-priced blankets.

The sight of so many wrapped-up passengers evoked a ghoulish image—a giant metal coffin, full of mummies, ready for burial. Any subsequent accident investigation would get sidetracked for weeks trying to come up with an explanation for the peculiar find.

Despite their limited mobility, the bundled-up passengers still somehow managed to send out messages on their devices to loved ones rather than prepare for ditching.

Noelle called the cockpit in desperation. “Mark, you’ve got to help me. No one is preparing for ditching back here. They’re all online. I know since 9-11 you can’t come out of the cockpit to deal with passengers, but *please do something*.”

Mark reached up to the overhead panel and flipped a switch labeled INTERNET. All activity on the passenger’s electronic devices came to a grinding halt.

The salesman looked up from his smartphone. “Hey, what happened? I lost my connection.”

Jan Frey begged, “I need the Wi-Fi! I didn’t finish my message to my kids!”

“Everyone, *please*, you must prepare for ditching. Put on your life vests and stow your belongings,” Noelle implored.

The nerves of the frightened passengers were understandably frayed.

Larry, the retired Tech Aerospace chief engineer, pointed at the Silicon Valley techies. “You’re the geeks who programmed this plane, right?”

One of them held up his hands in defense. “Easy, bro, we just—”

Larry cut him off before he could blurt out some lame excuse. “You guys were on your laptops when our plane went off course. What did you do? Is there something you’re not telling the crew? Us?”

“Hey, chill out, old man,” he rudely responded.

Larry glared at the arrogant geek.

Jan, Larry's seatmate, jumped to his defense. "Don't tell him to chill out. Answer his question. Why are we hopelessly off course? You wrote the code."

"They wrote every last line of it," Larry spitefully added.

A third techie chimed in. "Dude, we were playing Flight Simulator 10, okay?" He held up his laptop and proudly added, "I got high score. I made it to captain level."

The first techie clenched his teeth and glared at his buddy. "Shut the hell up!"

The last strands of civilized behavior finally snapped.

The salesman jumped up and ripped the laptop away from the clueless geek, smashing it on the floor. He hauled the scrawny geek out of his seat by his T-shirt and decked him. A full-on brawl broke out in the aisle as passengers jumped into the scrum. Others feverishly tried to break up the fight. The salesman was finally pulled off the bruised and battered techie.

Noelle screamed into the PA microphone, "Enough! You're behaving like wild animals! Everyone get back in your seats!" The combatants paused. One look at the expression on Charlotte's face, as she clutched a fire extinguisher, was all the motivation passengers needed. They drifted back to their seats, embarrassed by their behavior. Score: Wild Animals 1, Intelligent Humans 0.

Held back by other passengers, the salesman pointed at Noelle and demanded, "I want to know what the hell is really going on. What aren't you telling us?" Other passengers yelled the same thing. They wanted the truth.

Noelle responded, "Please, the captain has a plan to get us down safely. We have to trust him."

In reality, the passengers had no other choice than to accept Noelle's answer. The minute the aircraft door was closed back at JFK, control over their fate had been placed in the captain's hands—a total stranger.

The inebriated salesman slumped back down into his seat and started sobbing. "I don't want to die...I don't want to die." He was voicing what everyone on the plane felt.

Despite the trouble he'd caused, Noelle felt empathy for the frightened man. She walked over and gently patted his arm. "We're doing everything we can to get you down safely, sir." Although not nurses, like in the early days of airline travel, flight attendants were still expected to cure any problems their passengers had. She scanned the cabin full of anxious and frightened faces. All eyes were locked on to her, desperate for answers and comfort. If only comforting them was as easy as hugging her daughter and stroking her hair after a bad nightmare. But this nightmare was real. The incredible responsibility that came with the job was never more apparent to Noelle.

As she looked around the cabin, Noelle noticed the Russian acting particularly agitated. His ruddy complexion had turned pasty white, and he was sweating profusely. She started his way to see what she could do to calm him. Suddenly, the man jumped out of his seat, yelling something in his native tongue. He bolted toward the front door where Charlotte was standing and knocked her aside. It didn't take an interpreter to figure out his intentions. He grabbed the handle and tried to open the door. "I must get out of plane! I must!"

Extreme stress had overactivated his sympathetic nervous system and triggered his fight-or-flight response. This lead to an irrational attempt at escaping the inescapable. A short man in the front row lunged at the Russian, trying to stop him from opening the door. He pleaded with Charlotte to help him restrain the suicidal Slav.

Despite being equal in size to the burley Russian, Charlotte did absolutely nothing to intervene. Instead, she crossed her beefy arms and said, "Ivan, do you have a screw loose or what? As long as this plane is pressurized, Hercules himself couldn't open that door." She pointed down the aisle. "Go sit your sorry bee-hind down before I smack you upside the head!"

Despite the language barrier, the Russian understood the gist of Charlotte's reprimand. He came to his senses and abandoned his futile attempt to escape. The embarrassed Russian slinked back to his seat. Score: Wild Animals 1, Intelligent Humans 1.

Noelle walked over to the flight attendant panel and picked up the PA microphone. She tried her best to sound authoritative yet comforting. "Everyone, *please*, you need to get ready. There isn't much time left."

CHAPTER 33

A GROWING CROWD crammed into the small break room to watch the latest news reports. On one of the TVs, a blonde anchor held her finger up to her earpiece. "Hold on... Oh my God! I'm being told that all messages from the Tech-Liner passengers have suddenly stopped. We're still trying to get confirmation from the airline as to why, but our sources say they fear the worst might have just happened."

Peter Mills forced his way through the crowd then bolted from the room.

IN HER DORM room, Mary heard the same shocking report on her small TV. She shrieked in pain, pitched the remote at the wall, and buried her head in her hands, sobbing hysterically.

MILLS DARTED INTO the temporary command post. "Please tell me you have something."

Agent Janik jumped up from her desk and pointed at her laptop screen. "Got her! Margaret Larson, twenty-four, graduated from Amherst College. Majored in computer science. Minored in Middle Eastern studies. Estranged from her parents after converting. Recently moved to New York from Canada. Sitting in seat 7A." Justifiably proud of her investigative skills, Janik did a pull-down victory pump with her arm. "Boom! We got you now, you bastard." She stood on her tip toes and high-fived the taller Hawkins.

Ahmed sat back and calmly replied, "Never heard of her."

"Nice try, Einstein." Janik turned the laptop screen around. "Then why is she kissing you?" The selfie of Ahmed and Larson embracing on her Facebook page put the last nail in Ahmed's coffin.

Janik couldn't resist twisting the knife a little on the arrogant mechanic. "She's gonna be pissed when we tell her you gave her up in a heartbeat to save your own skin. Told us it was all *her* idea."

Ahmed lunged at Janik. "You bitch!" Cortez and Hawkins tackled him and shoved him back into his chair. Ahmed quickly regained his composure and arrogance. With a smug look on his face, Ahmed crowed, "You're too late anyway. She accomplished our mission. They'll never make it to the Azores. Allah will reward her a thousand times over for killing that Sunni dog Basara and striking a fatal blow against his wicked country."

Cortez, the battle-hardened former Marine, was dumbfounded. "That's what this was all about? You'd kill an entire planeload of innocent people to get revenge on some spoiled Saudi prince because he practices a different sect of Islam?"

"All Saudi infidels deserve to die for adopting the immoral ways of the West! They stole our land! They enslaved my people!"

Hawkins ridiculed Ahmed's logic. "Your people? Your mother emigrated from Iran when she was a kid. You were born and raised in New York, with a privileged upbringing on the Upper West Side. What the hell is wrong with you?"

Janik added, "So you sent your *girlfriend* on a suicide mission to do your dirty work? You friggin' coward."

Mills stroked his chin, desperately searching his memory. "Margaret Larson? Why does that name seem...?" His eyes opened wide. "Oh my God!" He bolted from the room.

As Mills left, the guard from the security office ran in, breathless. "Agent Hawkins! We just found a man murdered in a closet at the back of the hangar. He's a mechanic." The guard held up a plastic ID card streaked with blood. "The name on his ID says Marvin Timmons. His throat was slit with a box cutter."

Everyone turned toward Ahmed. Perversely proud of his actions, a chilling smirk flashed across his face.

Cortez ordered the guard, "Secure the crime scene. No one goes near it. We'll be there in a minute."

"Copy that. I'm on it, sir." The guard saluted with the wrong hand then scurried out of the office.

Cortez walked over to the door and locked it. He returned to Ahmed, seated in the chair. Supervisory Special Agent Cortez looked carefully around the room. Satisfied there were no security cameras, he reared back and threw an arcing roundhouse punch squarely into Ahmed's jaw. The mechanic toppled backward out of his chair, ending up sprawled on the floor, holding his jaw and whimpering like a child.

Cortez stepped back, rubbed his knuckles, then barked, "Get this scumbag out of my sight." He turned to his comrades. "Hawkins, have them call the plane. Tell them the hacker is Margaret Larson—seat 7A. Janik, I want to know how the hell Larson got on that flight."

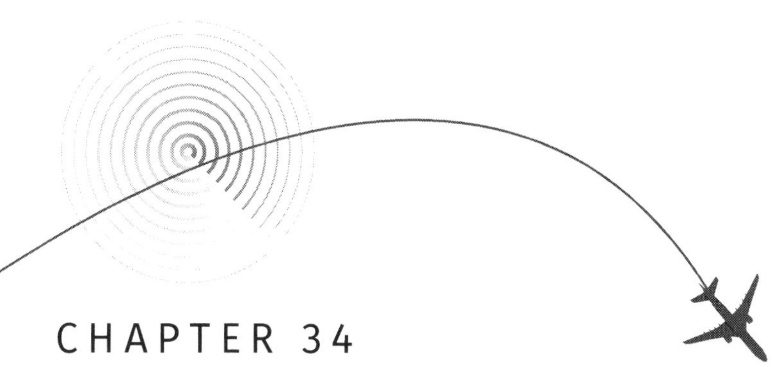

CHAPTER 34

THE POWERFUL SQUALL line was passing directly over the airport. The relentless rain came down in horizontal sheets, cutting the visibility to mere feet. Whitecaps lapped over the top of the protective seawall at the end of the runway. Emergency vehicles and personnel feverishly scrambled to set up.

Corey Thompson, Lajes Field fire chief, stood on the tarmac yelling into his handheld radio to be heard above the gale-force winds, "All units, this is Rescue One. Deploy the fire trucks evenly spaced down the runway. Medical, I need triage set up in one of the hangars. And where the hell is the Zodiac rescue boat?"

The beleaguered airport manager, standing next to Corey, apologetically said, "Sorry, Chief. Down for maintenance. It's in the shop."

Corey shook his head. He had taken this job a year ago looking for adventure and an easy way to earn tax-free income to supplement his meager monthly stipend from the Municipal Fire and Police Retirement System of Iowa. *So much for that plan.*

The airport's Rosenbaur Panther fire trucks, painted in high-visibility fluorescent yellow, sped off to their assigned spots next to the runway. The flashing red, blue, and white lights on the roofs of the trucks reflected off the low clouds, creating a strange discotheque-type light show.

Corey hurried out to the approach end of the runway in his fire-engine-red Range Rover command vehicle to orchestrate the firefighting efforts. He couldn't believe he was in this type of situation again. Once in a lifetime was once too often. Corey never expected to witness another horrible jet crash like the one he saw firsthand as a rookie fireman stationed at the airport in Sioux City, Iowa. The pilots flying a United Airlines DC-10 had miraculously made it to the runway with no functioning flight controls, only to drag a wingtip on touchdown. That sent the jumbo jet tumbling into a cornfield, engulfed in flames. To Corey's amazement, many of the passengers survived. *Would they be as lucky this time?*

Nighttime masked the violence of the storm engulfing the field. He stared intently through the rain-soaked windshield of his vehicle for any sign of the approaching jet. Corey leaned forward, blinking and squinting. He thought he saw a small change in the clouds. He stared harder. A faint light coming his way started to change the dark clouds at the end of the runway. The sound of a jet engine began to muscle aside the howling wind. Powerful landing lights on the approaching plane caused the clouds to glow even brighter.

Suddenly, the jet popped out of the clouds at the end of the field. It was wildly off course. The violently shifting winds were too strong. The plane was left of the runway and diving fast. Before the pilots could recover, the jet slammed into the ground and exploded in a massive fireball.

The flaming wreckage tumbled across the grass, bowling over a helpless police car, adding it to the conflagration. Before the plane even came to a stop, fire trucks rushed toward it across the muddy ground on their oversize all-terrain tires. Rolling up, the truck crews slewed their roof-mounted cannon turrets toward the wreckage and began spraying fire retardant foam toward the base of the flames. The veteran firemen dutifully doused the wreck, despite knowing in their hearts there was zero chance anyone could have survived such a horrific accident.

Corey skidded to a stop in his Range Rover as close to the flames as he dared. Peering through the windshield between wiper blade passes he noticed something odd. The smoking pile of wreckage was maybe four to five times larger than his Range Rover. The force of the impact was tremendous, but not enough to reduce a jumbo jet to such a small size. He got out and inched toward the flames. Toxic black smoke swirled around him, filling his lungs. He circled the wreckage, coughing violently until he was upwind and able to find fresh air. Corey turned his high-powered black Maglite flashlight on the wreckage. Despite the clouds of swirling smoke, two small jet engines, mounted on either side of the broken fuselage, under a T-tail, were clearly visible. He maneuvered around to get a better look at the tail which was tipped over at a forty-five-degree angle. The markings on it confirmed his suspicions: US Government Property – FBI. The Chief grabbed his handheld radio and screamed, "Redeploy! Redeploy! This isn't it! Get back to your positions!"

CHAPTER 35

WITH TEARS IN his eyes, one of the Silicon Valley techies leaned out into the aisle and flagged down a passing flight attendant. "Excuse me miss, do you have any paper?"

She looked at him with a confused expression. "Paper?"

"I want to write a goodbye note to my mom and...you know..." The flight attendant still looked confused. He spelled it out for her. "Tuck it in my pocket so the coroner will find it."

Her expression softened. Empathy for the young, frightened geek—the same age as her own son—kicked in. "I understand. Here..." She ripped a page out of her TECH-LINER EMERGENCY PROCEDURES MANUAL. "I won't be needing this anymore."

He sheepishly looked up at her. "And a pen?"

Noelle and Charlotte were bundled up tightly in their dark blue uniform overcoats—each garment a different size, of course. They worked together stowing away rolling carts in the forward galley. Charlotte turned to her friend. "Darlin', I don't know about you, but I'm scared. Real scared."

Noelle was surprised to see tears running down the cheeks of the toughest person she knew. She put her hand on Charlotte's arm. "Me too. More scared than I've ever been. I'll make you a deal. When we get to the Azores, I'll take you up on your offer to go to dinner. I'll spring for dinner at the best seafood restaurant on the island."

Charlotte crossed her arms and shook her head. "Hell no." Then she cracked a smile and said, "You make it chicken fried steak smothered in white gravy, and then maybe we have a deal."

Noelle grinned and nodded. "Deal."

Tina walked up with an apprehensive look on her face. "Um...Noelle?"

Great, just what I need right now. "Yes, Ms. Reynolds."

"I know I'm assigned to the jumpseat in the back of the plane, but..."

"But what?"

"Would it be possible...Could I...I don't know how to swim."

Noelle and Charlotte exchanged a look.

"Could I take a jumpseat up here instead?"

Charlotte looked at Tina's chest. "From the looks of it missy, you should float just fine."

Tina glared at Charlotte but held her tongue, aware her fate may rest on the sympathy of the woman's best friend.

Suppressing a laugh, Noelle was tempted to extract revenge on the platinum-blonde tart for tempting her man. But her conscience wouldn't let her. "I see. The jumpseat at the forward galley is open. You can take it. Stay close after we...Just stay close to me."

"Yes, ma'am."

THE COCKPIT SPEAKER crackled with an urgent message from dispatch. "Alpha One, this is Bill. We found the hacker on your plane. Her name is Margaret Larson. She is sitting in seat 7A."

Mark grabbed his mic. "We don't have time to confront her. We're approaching the airport. Pass the information along to the authorities. They can handle it if we...They can handle it."

"Roger, Alpha One. Will do."

Mark began to configure his plane in anticipation of reaching the runway. "Gear down. Flaps half."

Walter reached out and grabbed a metal handle with a small black plastic "tire" on the end, to extend the gear. "Jesus!" He jerked his hand away the handle as if it bit him. Every piece of metal on the plane was chilled so far below zero that touching it with bare skin burned like it was on fire. Losing fingers to frostbite was a genuine concern for the pilots. Walter took off his tie, wrapped it around his hand, then yanked the metal handle down. The massive landing gear swung down out of the belly of the plane into the windstream. Seconds later, the back edges of the wings extended out and down, allowing the plane to slow to a manageable speed for landing without stalling.

A flash of lightning suddenly filled the dark cockpit, momentarily blinding the pilots. Mark reached up and flipped a switch on the overhead panel, turning the cockpit lights on full bright. The bright light would help preserve their vision by forcing their pupils to constrict before the next lightning flash.

The storm violently battered the plane. Suddenly, it hit an air pocket, causing the plane to drop a hundred feet in less than a second. Screams from the cabin could be heard through the armored steel door.

Mark took control of the aircraft. "I'll take it from here, Walter." His numb fingers strained to grip the computer game-style control stick.

Walter shivered as he removed his right hand from his stick. Teeth chattering, he said, "Roger, you have the aircraft."

An alarm sounded in the cockpit. Showing no pity, the computer-generated female voice scolded the pilots again. *"FUEL LEVEL CRITICAL!!"* Powerless to change their fuel situation, they ignored the warning.

THE OCEANIC CONTROLLER radioed the plane. "Alpha One, you are entering Lajes tower airspace. Contact them on one two two decimal one. We'll monitor you until...we'll stay with you the rest of the way. Good luck."

The controller looked down at his hand, making sure he had released his mic switch. "Please, God..."

WALTER SWITCHED FREQUENCIES. "Lajes tower, this is emergency aircraft Alpha One, entering your airspace. We are lining up for landing on runway one five. Say visibility at the field."

Unaware of how critically short on fuel the plane actually was, the panicked tower controller responded, "Alpha One, this is Lajes tower. You are not cleared to land. I say again, you are not cleared to land. The field is experiencing a low-level wind shear and zero visibility. An inbound aircraft has just crashed on the infield. Go around! I order you to go—"

Mark reached over and switched off the radio.

Walter nodded in agreement.

The subzero temps inside the plane caused the cockpit screens to be obscured by a thin, milky-white layer of frost. Walter used his tie to wipe away an area big enough to see instruments vital to their approach. He called out the plane's current position, "We're a little left of course. Five miles to go. Runway not in sight."

Mark was laser focused on guiding the big jet, but staying on the correct course was very difficult. The turbulence tested Mark's skills as a pilot; just the sort of challenge an aviator normally relishes. But not today. Not now. They only had one shot at landing. There was no going around and coming back for another try.

THE ROUGH AIR jerked the plane up and down like an aerial roller coaster ride. Considering their long, gangly wings and almost football-field-length bodies, airliners can safely endure implausible amounts of turbulence. The passengers on board, not so much. The combination of a rough ride, rich food, and high levels of anxiety produced a predictable outcome. A few passengers grabbed for airsick bags tucked in the seat-back pockets in front of them. Violent retching quickly followed. When the nauseating smell reached the nostrils of nearby passengers, a chain reaction ensued.

THE INSTRUMENTS SHOWED the plane starting to sink. "Getting a little low on the glideslope, Mark."

"I know, I know." Mark tried to raise the nose of the jet to compensate. Every muscle in his body was shivering uncontrollably. The shaking was translating through the sensitive control stick, causing the jet to shake as well.

"Still below glideslope. Getting a little slow now."

Only one engine propelling the massive plane wasn't enough. "This isn't going to work. Gear up," Mark said.

Walter looked sideways at Mark. "Belly landing?"

"We're out of options."

Walter reached out and raised the handle. The gear tucked itself back into the body, greatly reducing drag. The plane rose back up to the proper glideslope.

The right engine coughed and sputtered, hungry for more fuel. That caused the output from the engine-driven electric generator to momentarily fluctuate. Lights in the cockpit and the three large screens flickered. Pressure in the lone hydraulic system powering the flight controls dipped also, causing the controls to become sluggish and ineffective.

Despite the extreme cold, a sheen of sweat formed on Mark's forehead. He commanded, "Deploy the RAT!"

The Ram Air Turbine was a small wind turbine that powered the minimum required electrical and hydraulic systems needed to maintain control during an emergency. Unlike the Auxiliary Power Unit (APU), a small jet engine that burns precious fuel, the RAT got all the energy it needed from the passing air.

Walter lifted a red-striped cover on the overhead panel and pushed the button under it. Below the plane, a small trap door opened. The RAT popped out into the airstream and rapidly spun up to speed. The lights and flight controls got a welcome reprieve from the backup power source, fully recovering.

IN THE CABIN, some of the passengers were quietly crying. Others were suddenly religious, mumbling prayers and blessing themselves with the sign of the cross, hoping for divine intervention. A few turned toward the techies and shot them evil looks, certain their youth and cockiness somehow contributed to the dire straits they were in. The temperature was comparable to a large walk-in freezer. Passengers could see the vapor from every breath they took—certain those breaths would be among their last.

Tina, wrapped in a blanket, made a final pass up the aisle. She checked passenger seat belts and life vests before heading for her jumpseat. A sudden jolt of turbulence levitated her off the floor, then slammed her down. Dazed but uninjured, Tina got up on all fours and crawled the last twenty feet to the jumpseat, securely belting herself in.

WALTER CLOSELY MONITORED the instruments for the one remaining engine. It had nothing left to give. The engine died out, suffering its own cardiac arrest. There was no training to fall back on in a situation like this. Mark was now in "command" of a seven-hundred-thousand-pound glider.

Walter dutifully stated the obvious. "That's it. We lost number two. Airspeed dropping. Getting low on glideslope. Half a mile to go. Still no runway in sight."

In a coldhearted voice, the computer announced over the cockpit speaker, "*Warning. Too low. Glideslope. Too low.*" They weren't going to make it to the runway.

Mark reached overhead and pulled out the circuit breaker for the incessant warning computer. He gently pulled back on his control stick, trying to extend the gliding distance. "Come on baby, just a little more."

"Lower the nose, Mark; we're gonna stall!"

"Come on! Come on!"

"Oh God. We're not gonna make it!" Walter grabbed the PA handset and screamed, "Brace for impact! Brace for impact!"

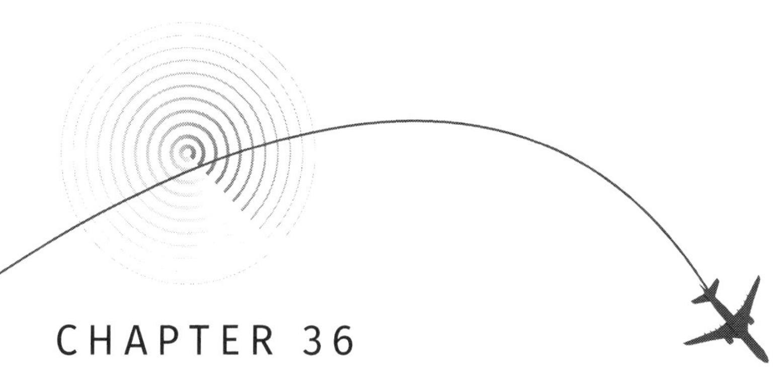

CHAPTER 36

FINE MOTOR SKILLS honed over forty years in the cockpit were put to the ultimate test. To extend their glide distance a few hundred more yards, Mark nudged his stick back mere millimeters. He forced the wings to give up their last bit of lift. It worked, but the Bernoulli principle didn't care if he was having a rough day.

"STALL!"

"STALL!"

"STALL!"

The Tech-Liner fell out of the sky as it crossed the end of the runway.

Its tail slammed into the raised seawall, completely shearing it off the back of the plane. The tail camera recorded every gut-wrenching second of the crash until its power cable was severed.

The tail hit caused the plane to pancake down hard onto its belly. The low-slung engines snapped off their wing-mounted pylons, disintegrating as they tumbled across the field.

The tremendous impact ripped Noelle's jump seat off its wall mounts—with her tightly strapped in it.

The crash unleashed mayhem in the cabin. To the terrified mind, it felt like a disaster movie in slow motion. Ceiling panels snapped loose and crashed down on helpless passengers below. Larry used his body as a shield to cover Jan. Contents from the overhead bins rained down into the aisles. Yellow emergency oxygen masks popped out of their overhead storage boxes, dangling like plastic spaghetti in front of the passengers.

The vacuum created by the air rushing past the gaping hole at the back end of the cabin sucked out all manner of swirling debris. Sounds from the terrified passengers were drowned out by the nails-on-the-blackboard shriek of the metal fuselage scrapping across the concrete runway.

The last row of seats in the cabin were now mere inches from the jagged back edge of the severed fuselage. Seat mounts attached to the weaken floor structure began to work themselves loose. Passengers in the last row grabbed at cables and hoses dangling from the damaged ceiling—anything that could be used as a lifeline.

A woman sitting next to the window clutched an orange hose dangling within reach just as her seat broke free from the floor. Her grip was no match for the five-hundred-pound seat she was tightly strapped to. The hose slowly slipped through her bloody hands as she cried out for help. Miraculously, the man across the aisle remembered the mind-numbing instructions given at the beginning of every flight. He reached over and lifted the metal tab on her seatbelt buckle to release it. She fell to the floor clutching the lifeline while her seat tumbled end over end out the back of the plane.

IN THE COCKPIT, Mark valiantly fought a losing battle with the ineffective flight controls. He was not going down without a fight. He slammed the control stick and the rudder pedals back and forth in vain, trying to direct the plane.

NOW RUDDERLESS, THE plane veered to the right and slid off the runway, narrowly missing a fire truck. It barreled toward the ramp lined with large hangars and the control tower. The controllers saw what was coming their way. They trampled over each other running for their lives. As it careened across the ramp, the Tech-Liner was on a direct collision course with a parked plane.

WALTER SCREAMED, "PLANE!" He crossed his arms in front of himself in a futile attempt to protect his body. It did little good. The impact with the parked plane crushed the right side of the cockpit as it ricocheted off the Tech-Liner, badly injuring Walter. His window shattered, spraying Walter with shards of razor-sharp glass. Ignoring his own safety, Mark reached over to stabilize Walter's bloody body.

AS THE PLANE slid across the tarmac out of control, the tip of its right wing sliced into a closed hangar door like a bayonet through flesh. The impact was enough to finally bring this terrifying, real-life version of Mr. Toad's Wild Ride to an abrupt end.

CHAPTER 37

WHEN THE PLANE came to a stop, an eerie silence filled the cabin. A few long seconds ticked by, then cries of joy erupted, followed by boisterous applause. The passengers couldn't believe it—they had made it to dry land. Strangers hugged one another, thankful to be alive. Laurent and his assistant passionately kissed.

With their lights flashing and sirens blaring, emergency vehicles swarmed the outside of the aircraft.

Charlotte unstrapped from her jumpseat and rushed over to help Noelle. "Hang on, honey, don't move. Help is coming."

Despite being injured themselves, the flight attendants limped into action. They manned their assigned doors and repeatedly yelled, "Unfasten your seat belts! Go to an exit! Jump!" The doors flung open, and warmer air flooded in. Emergency evacuation slides broke free from their door-mounted storage containers, then unrolled down to the ramp. In a matter of seconds, they inflated into rigid paths to safety.

In a heartwarming display of humanity, Larry, Jan, and other able-bodied passengers decided to stay on board and help the injured. Doctor Day pitched in. He ignored the bloody gash on his forehead and instructed the Good Samaritans.

The passengers were banged up, dazed, and bleeding—but thankful to be alive. Fractured bones, spinal injuries, and head wounds were gruesome evidence of the violence of the crash landing. Cries for help from the able-bodied passengers directed the rescue personnel entering the plane to the injured.

The nightmare for the battered passengers wasn't over yet. The rescue personnel had no choice but to triage the most seriously injured first. For now, a simple broken back would have to wait. If there was such a thing as a silver lining for the passengers on the Tech-Liner, with no fuel in the tanks, the risk of a lethal post-crash fire was off the table.

Although too early to contemplate now, in time, the passengers would form lifelong bonds of friendship because of the life-altering experience they had just survived.

MARK WAS FORTUNATE to come through the crash with only a superficial wound to his head. He stemmed the trickle of blood by pressing his handkerchief against the cut then unbuckled and reached over to steady Walter. As he reached out, Mark felt a sharp pain. It felt like an ice pick being thrust into his chest. Being slammed forward against his shoulder harness during the violent landing had likely broken a few ribs.

Walter was bleeding profusely. With so much blood, Mark couldn't tell from where. More emergency crews streamed into the airplane. Mark looked back and waved. "In here! He's bleeding. He needs a doctor!" An EMT heard his call for help and rushed into the cockpit carrying a large medical kit.

Mark continued to hold on tightly to his copilot while the EMT immediately started treatment. He said, "It's okay, Captain, I've got him. You can let go now."

Mark put Walter's life in the hands of the EMT. He turned to his copilot. "Hey, whiz kid, we did it. We made it to dry land. You're going home, Walter." In his typical dry sense of humor, Mark added, "Hopefully, the airline won't notice the small dents we put in the plane."

Walter winced as a smile emerged on his bloodied face.

Mark pointed the EMT toward Mo. "Please take good care of him."

The man looked over at Mo. He reached out and closed Mo's eyelids with the tips of two fingers to avoid the dead man's unnerving stare.

Mark left the cockpit to direct the evacuation, unsure how many, if any, of his passengers had survived.

THE SQUALL LINE had moved past the island. The wind and rain finally relented. Passengers slid down the emergency slides one by one into the welcoming arms of rescue personnel onto a wet, chaotic ramp. Military personnel, local police, and ambulance drivers pitched in to help comfort the dazed passengers.

Andrews and Hampton were among the first to evacuate but did nothing to assist the injured. Aware who the two men were, several passengers captured cell phone video of Andrews's and Hampton's cowardly behavior—soon to be shared with the whole world. When the pair put up their hands trying to block the cameras, they only dug their graves deeper.

Andrews separated from Hampton and was seen shortly after slapping François Laurent on the back and shaking hands—like someone applying for a job.

THE LAST OF the injured had been lowered to the tarmac by the rescue personnel.

Mark frantically searched the cabin for Noelle as the able-bodied passengers exited. He cupped his hands around his mouth and yelled, "Noelle! Noelle!" Mark stopped a flight attendant who was shepherding passengers. "Where's Noelle?"

"Sorry, Captain, I don't know." The flight attendant hurried away toward the front exit, yelling, "Leave all your belongings behind! Go to an emergency exit!"

The cabin was dimly lit by red and white emergency LED lights powered by their own internal batteries. The lights cast a strange glow on the unnerving scene. The devastation was incredible. Blood-streaked debris littered the cabin. That the body of the plane had stayed together in one piece, after *that* landing, was a testament to the skill of the structural engineers.

Mark fought through an obstacle course of dangling wires, mangled seats, and collapsed overhead bins, searching for Noelle and any remaining passengers. He yelled, "Is there anyone still on board? This is the captain! Yell if you can hear me!" He stopped and listened. No response came. Mark breathed a deep sigh of relief. All his passengers had safely evacuated.

He clawed his way back through the jungle of debris toward the front exit. As he neared the door, Mark stepped on a purse left behind by one of the passengers. He picked it up and opened the wallet inside. He hoped to find a name so he could return it to its rightful owner. He flipped through photos in plastic sleeves looking for an ID. Mark paused on a faded wallet-size picture of a couple on their wedding day. When he examined the picture more closely, his heart skipped a beat. He and Noelle were pictured kissing at the very moment the minister pronounced them husband and wife.

After all he had put her through, Noelle kept the photo in her wallet. The picture in the next sleeve showed Mary Smith beaming with excitement at her high school graduation, flanked by her proud parents. Mark clutched the wallet tightly against his chest as a tear ran down his cheek.

The flight attendant at the front door yelled, "Captain Smith!"

He looked up and saw her waving him toward the exit. Mark wiped the tear from his cheek. He walked up and handed her the purse. "This is Noelle's. Please safeguard it until I find her."

"Of course, Captain."

He motioned toward the slide. "That's everyone. Go." She jumped onto the slide and into the waiting arms of two fireman.

Mark turned and surveyed the carnage that used to be his airplane. He had no words for what he saw. Mark just shook his head in disbelief.

The white and red emergency cabin lights flickered, then extinguished. The Tech-Liner was dead.

Mark folded his arms across his chest, took one last look back, then jumped onto the slide—honoring the maritime tradition that the captain is always the last person to leave his ship.

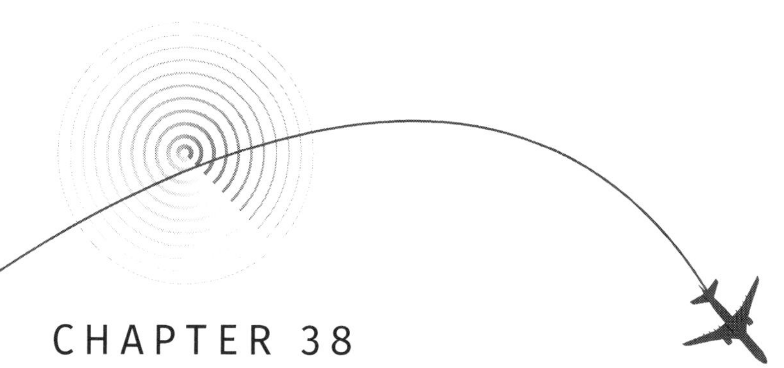

CHAPTER 38

FIRE CHIEF THOMPSON held his radio up to his mouth and announced, "Lajes tower, this is Rescue One. Send the following message to Gander Oceanic and Alpha Airlines. The plane made it. Numerous injuries. One flight attendant unaccounted for. All but one passenger survived."

"Roger, Rescue One. Glad to do it," the tower responded.

Mark walked the tarmac, stopping to check on his passengers as they received medical aid. He looked left and right, scanning the crowd, searching for Noelle. He yelled out in desperation, "Has anybody seen Noelle?"

Jan Frey ran up to Mark, choking back tears. "Thank you from the bottom of my heart for getting us down safely, Captain. Because of you I get to go home to my children and husband. I was sure I was never going to see them again." She gave Mark a heartfelt hug.

They certainly didn't train pilots how to handle this type of situation. Mark awkwardly responded, "You're welcome."

With tears streaming down her face, Jan hugged Mark even tighter. "God bless you."

He winced at the pain in his ribs from the bear hug but didn't dare complain.

Mark spotted Noelle across the ramp. She was being rolled away on a gurney, about to be put in an ambulance. Mark peeled the woman's arms from around his body. "I'm glad you're okay. If you'll excuse me..." He ran toward the ambulance, yelling, "Wait, wait!"

The ambulance attendant stopped when he saw Mark running his way. He asked Noelle, "Do you know him, ma'am?"

Noelle looked over and smiled. "Yes. He's my husband."

Mark sprinted up to Noelle's side. She was sitting upright on the gurney, her uniform covered with a wool blanket. Her right arm was bandaged up and immobilized between two stabilizing boards. Mark gently held her left hand. "Are you okay?" He turned to the attendant. "Is she going to be okay?"

"She'll be fine. A broken arm and a few lacerations. A day or two in the hospital, and she will good to go home."

Mark's heart was racing. "Everyone's been looking for you. We weren't sure you made it. Thank God you're alive."

"I'll be fine. Just a little banged up. Are all the passengers off the plane?"

"Yes, thanks to you and your crew." Mark caressed Noelle's left hand. He looked at the empty ring finger. The finger that once wore the pretty gold wedding band he took three weeks meticulously shopping for. The ring he had slipped on Noelle's finger when he pledged his eternal love for her. Mark's eyes started to mist up. "I thought I'd lost you for good."

Noelle smiled through the pain and looked across the scene. "From a little thing like this? You can't get rid of me that easy." They both laughed for the first time since...since either of them could remember.

Two FBI agents from the local office rushed up to Mark. "Are you the captain?" they asked in unison.

"Yes, who are you?"

The female flashed her badge. "Special Agent Crawford, sir. FBI. We know who the hacker is. Margaret Larson."

Noelle straightened up. "Margaret Larson? I recognize that name. She was sitting in seat 7A."

"That's right. Can you point her out to us?"

Noelle carefully scanned the crowded ramp. Larson was nowhere to be found. She closed her eyes to help block out the pain and focus her mind. *I was getting ready to confront the Russian about his laptop. The woman in 7A stood up and blocked my path. She put something in the overhead bin. It was a...*

Noelle's eyes opened wide. "A laptop bag! She was putting a laptop bag in the overhead bin!"

The male agent, Mitchel, asked, "Are you sure, ma'am?"

"Yes. The passenger in seat 7A has her own laptop bag."

He pointed back at the ramp. "Try again. Do you see Larson, ma'am?"

Noelle took a minute to meticulously search the ramp again. "No, I don't see her anywhere. I'm sorry." She plopped her head back on the gurney in frustration.

Mark jumped in. "Agents, she's been through a lot tonight. We need to get her to the hospital. Please, that's enough."

Agent Crawford took Noelle's left hand and slipped a business card in it. "Tomorrow, when you are feeling better, I want you to give me a call. Two of our fellow FBI agents died tonight trying to catch Margaret Larson. If there is anything else you remember—anything at all—please let us know. I want to nail that bitch."

Noelle looked up at Crawford. The fury burning in her eyes startled Noelle. "Absolutely. Anything I can do to help." As the agents started to walk away, Noelle bolted upright on the gurney and pointed across the ramp. "Wait! That's her! That's Margaret Larson!"

Margaret Larson, aka hippie chick, was limping in a hurry across the ramp, tightly clutching a laptop bag like it contained the Crown Jewels.

Mike Andrews saw her and waved. "Margaret! Wait up!"

She looked back, quickly looked away, and accelerated her pace.

The FBI agents raced over to Larson and seized her by the arms. Their desire to extract revenge for the fiery deaths of their Madrid-based comrades was palpable.

Larson tried to jerk her arms away. "What the hell are you doing? Let go of me." A crowd formed around the altercation.

Andrews walked up. "What are you doing? Unhand her."

Mitchel stepped in front of Andrews, blocking his path. He pulled his gold badge out of his pocket and thrust it in Andrews's face. "Agent Mitchel, FBI. Who are you? How do you know this woman?"

"I'm Mike Andrews, the CEO of Alpha Airlines. Margaret is my niece. I invited her on this flight as my guest. Why?"

Ignoring Andrews, he turned back to Larson. "You're under arrest for hijacking. Give me your bag." He yanked it out of her hand.

"That's my property! You have no right..."

He opened the bag, lifted the laptop out, and turned it over. On the back was written PROPERTY OF ALPHA AIRLINES. CONTROLLED ITEM. BRAIN KIT #3. MAINTENANCE USE ONLY. Agent Mitchel questioned Larson. "Is this your laptop, ma'am?"

Larson squirmed. "I must have accidentally taken it off the plane. That's not mine."

"Our computer forensics experts will get to the truth. Come with us."

Larson protested, "Wait! You're FBI. You have no jurisdiction here. I'm a Canadian citizen. The Azores has no hijacking laws on the books and no extradition treaty with the United States or Canada. Let go of me." She wrested her arms free from the agents. They reluctantly backed off.

Larson sneered. "Typical arrogant Americans. Just like you, your capitalist system is impotent and weak. I look forward to bringing it to its knees someday."

An Air Force colonel stepped out of the crowd. "Not so fast, ma'am." He pointed to the sign attached to the hangar, above the door with the Tech-Liner wingtip embedded in it. It proudly displayed the unit emblem for the 65th Air Base Group, US Air Force, Azores. He continued. "The concrete you happen to be standing on is considered sovereign territory of the United States under international law. I'm afraid you'll have to wait a little longer to bring down our corrupt system. I'd guess about ten to twenty years." The colonel pointed the FBI agents toward Larson. "She's all yours."

Crawford and Mitchel seized her again, barely restraining themselves from choking the life out of the arrogant little twerp right on the spot. "Margaret Larson, you are under arrest for the hijacking of flight Alpha One," Crawford said. "And for the death of the two agency pilots and two federal agents. You're going to fry for what you did, lady; along with whoever else helped you." The agents roughly marched her away.

Larson tried to stop them by planting her feet, but her slight build was no match for the stronger agents. She yelled, "Wait. Wait. Uncle Mike, help me!"

The agents yanked even harder.

As she was being hauled away, Larson could be heard shrieking something about her boyfriend, how he was the real mastermind, how she was just an innocent pawn, how...

Her pathetic attempts to shift blame could no longer be heard after she was tossed into the back seat of the agents' car and the door slammed shut in her face.

The Silicon Valley techies huddled together, pointing at the shrieking Canadian. They snickered to each other. "Poser."

A local policeman grabbed Andrews by the arm. "Her uncle, huh. Likely story. Sir, you'll need to come with me."

Andrews pleaded, "No, no, you misunderstand. I barely know her."

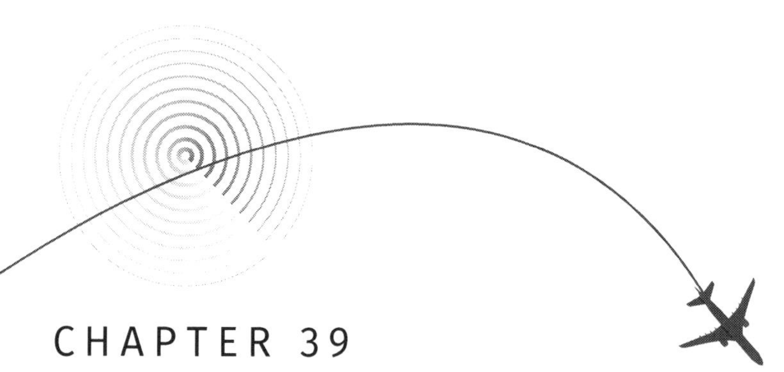

CHAPTER 39

MARK LOVINGLY HELD Noelle's hand. "Nice work, Purser."

She smiled. "Thank you, Captain."

Mark looked back at the barely recognizable plane, surveying the magnitude of the destruction before his eyes. He shook his head in disbelief, then looked at Noelle. "What the hell, maybe I'll go ahead and buy a boat after all. But only if you agree to be my copilot."

Noelle rolled her crystal blue eyes. "Copilot? I think I'd make a great captain."

Mark recoiled. "Two captains? That'll never work."

Noelle gave Mark a coy smile. "Who said anything about two?"

Mark knew better than to say a word. He just smiled, leaned down, and gave her a gentle kiss.

From across the ramp, Charlotte spotted Mark and Noelle. She smiled and waved. They both waved back. Tina meekly walked up next to Charlotte. She turned toward the blonde tart, planted her hands firmly on her hips, and poured on her Southern drawl extra thick, "Well, well. Looks like he's not available after all. *Honey.*"

As Noelle was being loaded into the ambulance, Mark's cell phone rang. He fished it out of his pocket and looked at the caller ID. "It's Mary." He flipped open the dated phone. "Hi, sweetie." Mark listened for a moment, then looked at Noelle while answering. "Yes, we're going to be okay."

A warm orange glow from the rising sun radiated from the eastern horizon. A new day was dawning for Mark and Noelle.

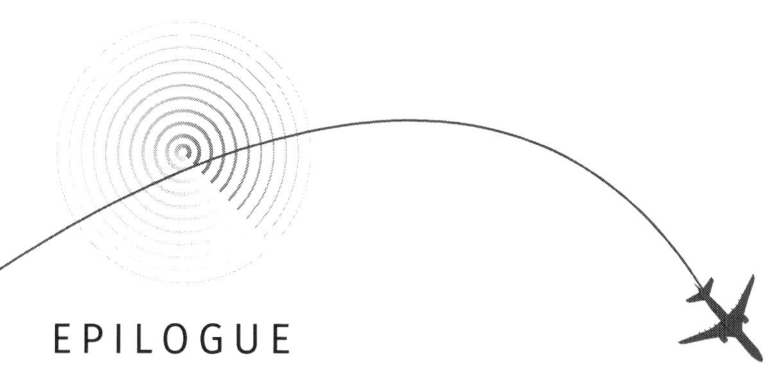

EPILOGUE

TWO DAYS LATER

"KNOCK, KNOCK, NOELLE. Prince Charming is here to see his Princess." Flowers in hand, a beaming Mark opened the door to patient room 132 at the Hospital de Santo Espirito da Ilha Terceira. To his embarrassment, Noelle was not alone.

Noelle's face lit up upon seeing Mark. "Good morning." She nodded to her right. "You remember the FBI agents from our little incident the other night—Agents Mitchel and Crawford."

The two agents held in a snicker as they shook Mark's hand.

"Agents. Good to see you again. How's the investigation going?"

"Larson is singing like a bird." Agent Crawford smiled broadly. "A little 'friendly persuasion' on my part, and she cracked like a walnut. We should have enough information about her boyfriend, Ahmed Harris, the mastermind behind all this, for an airtight case. My guess is he will be visiting one of our high-security facilities in Florence, Colorado for a long, long time."

Agent Mitchel frowned. "The only piece of the puzzle we can't quite figure out is the real role Mike Andrews played in all this. We're not buying his story he knew nothing about what his niece was up to."

Crawford added, "We'd like to hold him for another day of questioning, but unless we have some other lead to go on, I'm afraid he will get off scot-free."

Mark and Noelle looked knowingly at each other as if reading the other's mind.

Mark forced a concerned but helpful look. "I don't know if it would help your investigation, but why don't you tell the agents what Andrews said about his niece during the flight, Noelle?" He winked at her.

Noelle nodded knowingly. "Right...now don't quote me, but he said something along the lines of Larson always being his favorite niece and he pulled a lot of strings to get her on our flight."

Both agents scribbled furiously in their notebooks.

Noelle gladly continued. "It probably doesn't mean what it appears to mean. We're probably reading too much into what he said."

"We'll be the judge of that," Agent Crawford barked.

With karma fully locked and loaded, Mark quickly said, "I'm sure Noelle's doctor wouldn't want her to experience any more stress than absolutely necessary. Can we wrap this up?"

Agent Mitchel said, "Of course, we understand. You've both been very helpful." He shook Mark's hand and turned to leave.

Agent Crawford nodded gratefully toward them. "Thank you for all of your help, Ms. Parker..." Then she smirked. "And Captain *Charming*." She turned and walked out of the room.

Noelle shook her head and laughed. "We're terrible."

"We'll be long gone before they're finished with Andrews. Serves him right."

Noelle furrowed her brow. "I'm not sure how I feel about getting on a plane so soon, Mark."

"Don't worry, it's going to be a long time before I set foot on a plane myself. I booked a spare cabin for us on a cargo freighter, the *Lynda Ray*, sailing tomorrow for New York."

"You? On a boat?"

"I figured if I'm going to begin a new chapter in my life, I might as well start turning some pages. A boat ride back home sounded like a nice, boring way to begin."

"Good for you, Mark. Count me in."

"Knock, knock." A dark-haired man in a white coat appeared at the door. "Good morning, Noelle."

"Doctor Ferreira, please come in."

The obviously smitten doctor waked up to her bedside. "And how is my lovely American patient feeling this morning?"

"No offense to your wonderful hospital, Doc, but I'm ready to go home."

"I completely understand." He looked suspiciously at Mark. "And who might you be?"

Mark reached out to shake the doctor's hand. He introduced himself with an extra firm grip. "Mark Smith. I'm Noelle's *husband*."

The doctor's expression flashed to admiration. "Captain Smith, it's a pleasure to meet you. Our little island is all abuzz about what you pulled off the other night."

"Thanks. We were very lucky."

"That's not what Noelle tells me."

Noelle caressed Mark's hand then asked, "So...are you going to let me go home, Doc?"

"Reluctantly, yes. I'm discharging you this morning. You are free to go. Just take it easy on that arm for six weeks."

"Yes, sir." Noelle gave a mock salute with her left hand, since her right arm was encased in a fresh white cast.

"I assume you'll be catching the first flight out of here?" the doctor inquired.

Mark spoke up. "We've both decided it will be a while before either of us gets on another plane. We're catching a boat tomorrow bound for New York. A relaxing ride home sounded like just what the doctor ordered. Wouldn't you say so, Doc?"

The doctor frowned. "Well, *Doctor* Smith, in my professional opinion—based on *actually* attending medical school"—his frowned reversed—"your prescription is right on the money. My best to both of you. Bon voyage." With that, the doctor turned and left.

Noelle looked up at Mark. "How's Walter doing?"

"He should be coming out of surgery right now. His doctor said he'll be here for a few more weeks. His wife flew in last night to stay with him until he gets out. Unfortunately, he'll never fly again."

"Let's stop by his room on our way out. I want to thank him for what he did."

NEXT MORNING

A UNIFORMED CREWMAN, clipboard in hand, greeted them as they reached the top of the gangplank. "Welcome aboard the *Lynda Ray*. Names, please."

"Mark and Noelle Smith." Noelle beamed and linked her good arm through Mark's.

He thumbed through the manifest. "Smith...Smith; here you are. Cabin number three." He pointed. "Go down this hallway. Your room will be on the left."

AS THEY GOT settled into their spartan cabin, there was a knock at the open door. A gray-bearded man in a double-breasted black uniform with gold buttons stood in the doorway. "Allow me to introduce myself. I'm Captain Oliveira. My first mate tells me we have a hero on our humble ship today."

Mark blushed. "I was just doing my job, Captain Oliveira. I'm sure you've had your share of hairy situations during your career. Thank you for allowing us to ride along with you to New York, sir."

"It's an honor to have you both aboard. Our trip will take four days, so if there is anything you need during our voyage don't hesitate to ask. My ship is your ship."

"Thank you. That's very kind of you," Noelle responded.

He tipped his cap. "Captain Smith. Ma'am."

TWO DAYS LATER

MARK AND NOELLE were topside leaning against the railing, looking out on the vast ocean. The ship was rhythmically swaying with the waves, which had gradually increased in height since leaving port.

Mark had his arms wrapped tightly around Noelle's slender waist. The strained expression on her face concerned Mark. "Are you OK? The waves bothering you?"

"No, it's not that."

"What is it then?"

"I'm really worried about Mary. When we called her from the hospital she was so upset. I need to hug her, tell here everything's going to be okay. I just wish there was some way we could talk to her."

"We'll arrive in New York in a couple of days. You'll get to see her soon." Mark could tell from the look in Noelle's eyes that waiting until they arrived in New York to see their only child was not going to cut it. Noelle needed to satisfy her protective mama bear instincts and allay any fears their daughter might have had as she anxiously awaited their return.

Noelle pressed her body closer to Mark. In her sweetest voice, she asked, "What if you talked to Captain Oliveira? Asked him if there is any way we could call Mary from his ship?" She was no amateur when it came to getting Mark to do what she wanted when it was important to her. Those seductive eyes, and that smile, with just the right amount of pouting mixed in, were more than the strongest-willed man could resist.

Mark's reluctance to play the captain card to get the *Lynda Ray's* skipper to bend the rules, as a professional courtesy, evaporated the instant he looked at Noelle. "Ships are connected to a nautical satellite communications network. No promises, but I'll ask the captain if he would be willing to let us make a *short* call on it. Head back to our cabin. I'll go ask."

"Ships can make phone calls? I didn't know that." Noelle hid her smile, letting Mark think he was the smart one.

LATER

"THANK YOU AGAIN, Captain Oliveira, for allowing us to call our daughter. My wife and I greatly appreciate it," Mark said sheepishly.

The captain looked over at Noelle and Mark from his chair on the bridge with a tight smile. "No bother at all, Captain Smith. Having been married for over forty years, I know how persuasive a wife can be when it involves her children." He shot Noelle a sideways glance. "My communications officer will assist you with your call. I ask that you limit it to ten minutes, though."

Noelle reached out and shook Oliveira's hand. "Thank you, sir. Ten minutes. Not a minute more. We don't want to keep you from your important duties commanding this impressive ship."

Captain Oliveira half smiled and nodded, knowing full well he was being flattered by a pro. "COMMO, establish a connection with the Iridium system," he commanded.

"Aye aye, sir." The communications officer walked over to a panel covered with knobs, buttons, and displays. Mark and Noelle watched as he reconfigured the satellite communications system to connect into the terrestrial phone network. He instructed Noelle, "Okay, dial the phone number like you would at home except add 001 plus the area code."

Noelle dialed Mary's cell phone.

After a few rings she picked up. "Hello?"

"Hi sweetie, it's Mom and Dad."

"Mom? Is there something wrong? I thought you were on a ship headed for New York."

"We are. Everything's okay. The nice captain on our ship has graciously allowed us to make one quick phone call from the cockpit."

Mark nudged her, looking embarrassed. "Bridge. It's called a bridge."

Captain Oliveira shook his head.

Noelle blushed. "Anyway, I couldn't wait two more days to see you and give you a big hug, so we're calling to make sure you are okay. How are you doing?"

"I'll be honest, Mom, it's been a rough couple of days. Watching your terrifying flight unfold live on TV, then wondering if I'd ever see you guys again; it's been a lot to process. The school counselor has been very supportive helping me work through my feelings. She said I just have to give it some time. But enough about me. How are you guys doing?"

Mark chimed in. "It'll be a while before we get on another airplane, that's for sure." He hesitated, then said, "Mary, we have something important to tell you. Your mother and I have decided to give our marriage another try."

Silence from the other end.

"Mary?"

"That's great. Um..."

Mark and Noelle look suspiciously at each other.

"I have some important news I need to tell you guys, also. And Dad, please don't be mad."

Mark furrowed his brow. "Mad about what?"

"I've...I've decided to take this semester off from med school."

Silence from this end.

"Mom? Dad?"

Using all the self-restraint Mark could muster up, he held back giving his opinion on his daughter's rash decision. He gritted his teeth. "Go on."

"I talked to the dean, and he said he completely understands, given what happened. He said they would welcome me back with open arms next semester."

"What prompted this big decision, sweetie?" Noelle asked.

Mark and Noelle could hear Mary start to choke up. She drew in a long breath. "I want us to be a real family again. Like it used to be before the...like it used to be. I wasn't there for you guys like I should have been when things got rough between the two of you. I want to try to make up for lost time. Work on that parent/daughter bonding thing Dad always talks about."

Time flew by as Mark, Noelle, and Mary started to take initial steps toward repairing their broken family.

Twenty minutes into the call, Oliveira frowned at Mark and impatiently tapped the face of his wristwatch.

Mark got the message. "Sweetie, we need to wrap this up. Mom and I will see you when we dock in New York."

They both said in unison, "We love you."

Mary said the same.

Noelle and Mark thanked the captain profusely and quickly exited the bridge before they imposed any more on the crew.

Oliveira scowled as he looked at his crew. "Anyone who mentions this to the company will be walking the plank. Understood?" he said menacingly.

The entire crew quickly nodded in understanding.

"COMMO, return the comm system to normal monitor frequency."

As soon as the officer switched the panel back to the proper frequency, an urgent radio call blared from the speaker. "Vessel *Lynda Ray*, this is the National Weather Service Maritime Weather Office. How do you copy?"

The communications officer responded, "National Weather Service, this is the *Lynda Ray*. Go ahead. Over."

The irate radio man on the other end barked, "Where the hell have you guys been? I've been trying to call you for the last ten minutes."

Oliveira waved off his comm officer and took the mic. "National Weather Service, this is the captain. Our comm system was experiencing a small problem. We had to take it offline for a few minutes. Go ahead with your message."

"*Lynda Ray*, the tropical depression east of Bermuda we told you about yesterday has tripled in strength overnight and has switched to a northeasterly track. A Category 3 hurricane is barreling directly toward you!"

ABOUT THE AUTHOR

DAN STRATMAN IS a retired major airline Captain with over 26 years of experience in the industry. Before flying for the airlines, he was a decorated Air Force pilot. In addition, Captain Stratman is a highly sought-after aviation consultant, media aviation spokesperson, and NASA Astronaut applicant. He is a World traveler, having been to 38 countries so far.

The MAYDAY! story was originally written as a screenplay. After it did well in several large screenplay competitions, Dan thought it would be well-received by a wider audience and decided to convert it into a novel.

Dan has an entrepreneurial side that stretches back many years. He developed the popular air travel app, Airport Life. The app did something that was sorely needed, it made flying easier and less stressful for passengers. In addition, he created a specialty photo printing eCommerce website, ran a multi-expert aviation consulting company he founded, and has filed numerous patents. In his spare time Dan enjoys mentoring budding entrepreneurs and volunteering weekly with Habitat for Humanity.

The two things he is most proud of are his long marriage to his lovely wife and his three wonderful kids.

Made in the USA
Monee, IL
12 June 2023

35692296R00164